CONAN DOYLE MYSTERIES

For Elizabeth – the very best of companions

Kelpies is an imprint of Floris Books
First published in 2018 by Floris Books
© 2018 Robert J. Harris

Robert J. Harris has asserted his right under the
Copyright, Designs and Patent Act of 1988 to be
identified as the Author of this Work

This publisher acknowledges subsidy from
Creative Scotland towards the publication
of this volume

 Also available as an eBook

British Library CIP data available
ISBN 978-178250-483-2
Printed & bound by MBM Print SCS Ltd, Glasgow

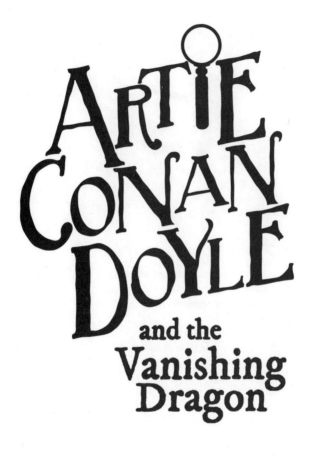

ARTIE CONAN DOYLE

and the
Vanishing
Dragon

ROBERT J. HARRIS

Kelpies

MR ROBERT J. HARRIS
in association with
KELPIES PRODUCTIONS
presents:

The Vanishing Dragon

A SPECTACULAR NEW SHOW FEATURING:

THE GREAT WIZARD OF THE NORTH
Professor John Henry Anderson

THE THEATRICAL PHENOMENON
Miss Rowena McCleary

THE FEARLESS DETECTIVES
Mr Artie Conan Doyle and
Mr Eddie 'Ham' Hamilton

Kairos
Pharaoh of the Fantastic

The Psychic Marvel
Miss Louise Anderson

The Dancing Nymph
Mademoiselle Delphine

Madame Sophonisba
Priestess to the Goddess Astarte

THE SUPPORTING CAST INCLUDES:

Sir Merriot 'Red-Faced' Ruthven   Mr Charles and Mrs Mary Conan Doyle

Lady Winderbrook 'The Bird'   Berrybus the Mighty Hound

PLUS A SPECIAL GUEST APPEARANCE BY THAT POPULAR POLICEMAN:
Sergeant George McCorkle

1.

An Invitation to Magic

Edinburgh, July 1872

"Detectives, that would be the life for us," Edward Hamilton announced suddenly.

Artie Conan Doyle looked up from his Latin textbook and gave his friend a puzzled frown. "Ham, what on earth are you talking about?"

"I'm talking about the future," said Ham. "I've been thinking a lot about it lately. My mother says now that I've turned thirteen I'm well on my way to being a man. I need to consider my future career."

They were seated on the floor of Artie's cramped bedroom at Sciennes Hill Place with their textbooks in their laps. Artie had a notepad in which he was scribbling a rough translation of the page they were working on. A large Latin dictionary lay on the floor between them.

"Why would we want to be policemen?" said Artie distractedly, running his finger along the next line in the text.

"No, not policemen," said Ham. "We'd be independent consultants with our own office and everything."

"Can I consult you now and ask you to look up the meaning of the word *ferentes*?" Artie pointed at the dictionary.

With a sour look Ham opened the large book and began flipping through the pages. "The point I'm making, Artie, is that we need to start planning ahead." A gleam appeared in his brown eyes. "I've been thinking, you know, about that business with the Gravediggers' Club."

A few months before, the boys had solved a mystery involving grave robberies and some unsavoury villains. It had all turned out well in the end, in spite of some terrifying moments.

In the following months life had returned to its normal routine, and as he read a tale of the heroes of the Trojan War for his Latin homework, Artie couldn't help yearning for some adventure, some new mystery, to enliven his world. He knew, however, that with his older sister Annette away at school in France, it was up to him to support the family through his father's frequent bouts of illness. He couldn't manage that by daydreaming.

"That was something we just stumbled into," he told Ham abruptly. "What has that got to do with our future?"

"Well," said Ham, "we solved that mystery, didn't we?

Don't you suppose somebody might pay us to solve other cases?"

Artie couldn't help scoffing. "Why on earth would anybody pay us to solve a mystery? They could do it for themselves. Or just go to the police."

"They might not be clever enough to solve it themselves," Ham insisted. "And as for the police, they didn't seem particularly bright last time. Plus, suppose it's a delicate matter that a person might not want to take to the police. That's where we would come in – Hamilton and Doyle, Consultative Investigators."

"Hamilton and Doyle?"

"Alright, Doyle and Hamilton if you like."

"As I recall, I had to drag you into that business of the gravediggers," Artie reminded his friend. "You weren't at all happy tramping around graveyards."

"Well, we could make it a rule not to take on any cases involving dead bodies," said Ham very seriously. "We could be more exclusive. And that would still leave burglaries, blackmail and other stuff."

For a moment Artie felt a stir of excitement at the thought. But no, he had responsibilities and for the sake of his family he had to be practical.

He shook his head firmly. "Look, Ham, nobody is going to hire a couple of amateurs for serious business like that."

"They do in America," Ham countered. "I read about that chap Allan Pinkerton who set up a detective agency over there, and he's Scottish like us."

"America is different," Artie argued. "There are so many bandits and outlaws over there, they need all the help they can get. Over here, there's simply no demand. No, I can't say this idea of yours appeals at all."

Ham cast a longing glance at the window and sighed. Outside the streets of Edinburgh were thronged with people enjoying the sunshine. "You know, Artie, I don't see what use all this Latin is going to be to us – not unless we decide to become priests." He made a face. "And I don't fancy that much. Black's not my colour and I can never remember the right words to all those prayers."

"Well, a lot of Latin terms are used in medicine and in the law," Artie pointed out.

Ham shook his head. "No, I don't see me being a doctor or a lawyer."

"I don't see you being much use to me either," said Artie, "if you don't look up *ferentes* like I asked you to do."

Book 2 of Virgil's *Aeneid*, the epic Roman poem containing the tale of the wooden horse of Troy, had been set as part of their homework for the summer break. Both were pupils at Stonyhurst College in Lancashire and even though the boys were back home in Edinburgh, the school demanded that they keep up their studies.

Reluctantly Ham consulted the dictionary. "It means… *bringing* or *bearing*."

"Right." Artie scribbled in his notepad. "*Greeks bearing gifts*." He looked up at his friend. "I thought your mother had your future planned out, Ham."

Ham rolled his eyes. "She wants me to follow a career in music, just because *she's* a piano teacher."

"What's wrong with that?" asked Artie.

"You know how little money she makes. Sometimes she even has to take in laundry to make ends meet. Besides, I can't imagine anybody paying to listen to me play the piano. She's been forcing me to bang out some sonatas and keeps telling me how well I'm doing, but I can hear for myself that it's a beastly racket."

"Maybe you just need more practice," Artie suggested.

"What would be the point? You see all those ragged chaps on the street playing fiddles and organs for pennies – they probably started out hoping for a magnificent musical career, and look what they've sunk to."

"I shouldn't worry about it, Ham. I expect something will turn up in due time."

"I don't agree, Artie." Ham wagged his finger exactly like Father Cassidy, one of their Jesuit teachers, did when making a serious point about religion. "Real life isn't like those stories you're always reading where some chap is snatched up by a giant condor, dropped into a forest where he becomes the chief of a band of brigands, marries a princess and ends up as the ruler of Bangalore. You can't just count on luck coming your way."

Artie looked up sharply from his Latin text. "Captain Mayne Reid and Mr Fenimore Cooper's stories aren't nearly as silly as that," he protested, naming two of his favourite authors.

At that moment there came a loud knock at the front door.

"I'd better get that." Artie rose to his feet with a grunt. His parents and two younger sisters had gone out for the day, so there was no one else in the house.

Crossing the hallway, he opened the front door but there was nobody waiting on the landing. Instead he spotted an envelope lying at his feet. For a moment he was afraid it might be another bill, but when he picked it up he saw at once that it couldn't be.

The envelope was deep crimson with a thin gold border running around the edge. It was addressed in gold lettering to:

Master Arthur Conan Doyle
3 Sciennes Hill Place
Edinburgh

When Artie returned to his room Ham had pushed the dictionary away and was seated on the edge of the bed swinging his legs. "I say, that's jolly important-looking," he said, hopping down to join his friend.

Artie took out his penknife and carefully ran the blade along the top of the envelope, opening a neat slit. Poking a finger inside, he slipped the contents out.

"Well, how extraordinary!" said Ham.

Setting aside the empty envelope, Artie examined the two oversized playing cards he now held in his hand. One was the ace of diamonds, the other the eight of hearts, and on the back, rather than the abstract design he might have expected, were a pair of identical invitations:

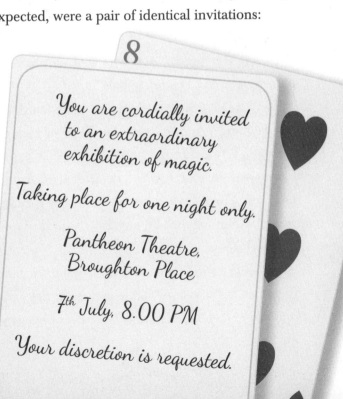

You are cordially invited to an extraordinary exhibition of magic.

Taking place for one night only.

Pantheon Theatre, Broughton Place

7th July, 8.00 PM

Your discretion is requested.

"Why, that's tonight," said Artie.

Ham craned in for a closer look. "What do you suppose it means: your discretion is requested?"

"I would guess we're not to tell anybody."

"That's a bit daft," said Ham. "Surely when you're putting on a show you want a big crowd to show up. How else will you make a profit?"

"This seems to be a very unusual show," said Artie, "and a private one. I can't think why I've been invited."

"Do you suppose it's a mistake?"

"Perhaps," said Artie. He was staring at the cards when a thought occurred to him. "The ace of diamonds, Ham, do you see?"

"See what?"

"**AC**e of **D**iamonds," Artie repeated, emphasising three of the letters. "ACD – my initials."

"Why yes!" Ham plucked the other card from his friend's hand. "And this one, the **E**ight of **H**earts. EH – that's me, Edward Hamilton."

"It seems too clever to be a coincidence." Artie rubbed his chin. "These invitations are definitely meant for the two of us. But why would anybody want us there, if this is so exclusive?"

Suddenly Artie felt the same excitement that had stirred him when he pondered baffling clues in the case of the Gravediggers' Club. The shabby walls of his tiny room, the piles of school books and everything else seemed to fade into the background as this new mystery filled his mind, like a blaze of sunlight dispelling a dull fog.

"The only way to find out is to go," said Ham. "Oh, Artie, I haven't been to a show in ages. They're so expensive and this is *free*."

"We have to go, of course," Artie agreed, "but my parents won't care for the notion of me being invited to a mysterious magic show by an anonymous stranger."

"We need a cover story." Ham pursed his lips in thought. "I know. Tell them an uncle of mine got these invitations, you know, as a late birthday present for me. That way it all sounds completely above board."

"And what will you tell your mother?"

"I'll tell her they came from an uncle of yours, of course. It's perfect."

Artie flipped his card over to read the invitation again and his jaw dropped. "Ham, look at this!"

Ham gaped and turned over his own card. "Artie, that's amazing!"

To their astonishment, the words on the back of each card had vanished. In their place was a large black question mark.

2.

The Curtain Rises

That evening a crowd of about a hundred people gathered outside the Pantheon Theatre. As it was summer it was still daylight, but that did nothing to lessen the air of mystery that hung over the occasion. A buzz of excitement ran through the crowd and many of them showed off the extraordinary playing cards they had received and speculated about how the magical effect of the disappearing words had been achieved.

The theatre was a modest building of white sandstone with a pair of Greek-style pillars supporting an arch over the main door. There were no posters or placards outside announcing a show, which made the event all the more intriguing. Shuffling their feet behind a tall man in a top hat and tails and a woman wrapped in a silk shawl, Artie and Ham looked distinctly out of place in their school uniforms.

"Why does everybody keep looking at us?" Ham muttered. "Are we not well enough dressed?"

"As well as we can be." Artie self-consciously straightened his tie. "I suppose they're wondering what two youngsters are doing here without an adult."

"I should think we're grown up enough to take care of ourselves," said Ham. "My mother says I'm quite the gentleman."

"I'm sure she does, Ham," said Artie.

He gazed around at the crowd, trying to discern something in common between them. Apart from the fact that they were obviously prosperous they appeared quite varied.

Nearby, a lanky young man in a blazer and flannels was joking with a girl who was busily fanning herself against the heat.

"It's probably going to be a demonstration of some new miracle elixir that cures every ailment," he suggested with a chortle. "And when the show's over we'll be expected to buy at least a dozen bottles each of the foul-smelling brew."

The girl gave him a playful slap on the shoulder with her fan. "You are awful, Gerald," she said primly. "I'm quite sure it will be something wonderful. Perhaps one of those oriental fakirs who can float off the ground while lying on a bed of nails."

"Did you hear that, Artie?" said Ham. "I don't like the sound of that. Suppose he lost control of the bed of nails and it fell on us."

"Whatever's going on, I'm sure it's all perfectly safe," Artie reassured his friend.

A white-haired man further down the queue gave a snort as he examined his pocket watch through the lens of his monocle. "It's a full minute after eight," he complained gruffly. "This had better not be some confounded jape."

"You see," said Ham, "I'm not the only one who's getting suspicious. I say, you don't suppose it could be some sort of a trap, do you?"

"Ham, what on earth are you talking about?"

"Well, why lure all these people here in secret? Maybe we're all going to be kidnapped."

"It would be a bit of a tall order to kidnap this many people," Artie pointed out.

"Pirates could do it. They'd be extremely fierce, armed with pistols and swords. I don't think they'd get much resistance out of this lot. They all look a bit soft, if you ask me."

"And what would these pirates do with us all?" Artie inquired dubiously.

"Well, once they'd finished robbing us, they'd probably hold us to ransom. That would be bad news for you and me, Artie. I don't think our families could raise much of a ransom. We'd probably be sold into slavery."

"Look on the bright side," said Artie. "If that does happen you'll never have to practise the piano again."

From up ahead came the sound of the doors opening and a thrill of anticipation passed through the crowd as everyone began to file into the theatre.

The foyer was lit by old-fashioned oil lamps and the faded posters on the walls were like something from a bygone age. One advertised a local singer whose name was long forgotten, and another an evening of Lancashire clog dancing.

A portly man with a drooping silver moustache checked that each of the boys had a special playing card, then an usher showed them to their seats.

The auditorium was equipped with red velvet seating for up to two hundred people, Artie estimated. By the time everyone was inside more than half the places were occupied, in the rows nearest the stage. He gazed around at the golden cherubs decorating the walls, their chubby faces framed by bird-like wings. Higher up the box seats appeared to be empty and directly overhead three crystal chandeliers shone down.

A plain red curtain hung across the stage and there was still no indication of who had organised the event.

"Tell me, my good man, don't you have any

programmes?" one gentleman demanded as the usher showed him to his seat.

"I assure you, all will be revealed shortly, sir," the usher replied politely.

Artie was seated three seats in from the central aisle, the two seats to his right being empty. On his left Ham was craning about looking at the faces of their fellow audience members.

"I don't think anyone we know is here," said Artie.

"Maybe not," said Ham, "but I swear some of these faces are familiar from the newspapers. That lady over there in the flowery hat is Evelyn Tancred, the singer. And I'm sure that chap over there played Hamlet at the Palace last year. What's his name? Gilbert something?"

Artie was distracted when someone suddenly plonked himself down in the seat by the aisle to his right. Unlike most of the audience, who had arrived in groups or pairs, he appeared to be alone.

The man was wearing a wide-brimmed hat and a pair of tinted glasses. The lower half of his face was concealed beneath a thick black beard. The fingers of his left hand drummed impatiently on the armrest and Artie observed that he was wearing an unusual ring on his middle finger. It looked like it was made of gold and it was decorated with a triangle, from the centre of which a small green jewel glinted like a tiny eye.

The man glanced in Artie's direction and when he saw the boy gazing at the ring he thrust his hand into his pocket, as though he had been caught stealing something.

The thought flickered across Artie's mind that there was something decidedly odd about the stranger, but he supposed there were all sorts of unusual people in the world of magic.

The orchestra pit in front of the stage was sunk so low that Artie could only see the tops of the musicians' heads. When they began tuning up, it stirred renewed excitement in the audience.

Silence fell, however, when the house lights dimmed and the portly man from the foyer appeared in the centre of the stage. He paused, assuring himself that every eye in the house was fixed upon him, then cleared his throat and spoke.

"Ladies and gentlemen, honoured guests, I am Montague Ruff, the theatrical manager, and tonight it is my privilege to introduce to you a man whose name is legend across the globe, from Glasgow to Cairo, from the Firth of Forth to the Gulf of Mexico. He has turned tigers into goldfish, trapped the devil in a bottle, and made a stage full of dancing nymphs vanish into thin air."

The audience murmured guesses about whom the

subject of this extravagant praise might be. The man on stage gestured dramatically as he continued.

"He has baffled his peers with extraordinary effects. He has rendered the crowned heads of Europe stunned and amazed. Without further ado, I present to you Professor John Henry Anderson – the Great Wizard of the North!"

"Professor Anderson!" Ham gasped. "Artie, this is better than I could have dreamed! He's... why, he's..."

"He's the greatest magician alive. I thought he was retired."

"Not any more," said Ham excitedly.

The orchestra struck up a spirited march – and the curtain rose.

3.

Enter the Great Wizard

The curtains opened to reveal a row of huge playing cards, each as big as a door, lined up at the back of the stage with the king of clubs in the centre. Directly in front of the king, with his back to the audience, stood a tall figure draped in a long black cloak with a top hat covering his head.

The audience began to clap, for this was surely the celebrated magician himself. Everyone leant forward, waiting for him to turn around. The figure on the stage, however, remained completely motionless.

Just as the applause faded, from inside the cloak came a loud *boom* and a billow of crimson smoke. The cloak dropped to the floor and the top hat flew high in the air. At the same instant, a man in dapper evening dress burst through the giant king of clubs card.

He caught the top hat as it fell, plopped it on his head then, stooping only slightly, whipped the cloak off the floor and swept it around his shoulders. Advancing to the front of the stage, he stretched out his hands to the audience, who broke into thunderous applause, cheers and whistles of approval.

Removing his hat, the magician bowed deeply then tossed his hat aloft. As it sailed towards the rafters, it disappeared in a puff of white smoke, leaving behind a live dove flapping in the air. The dove circled once over the heads of the crowd then vanished behind a side curtain.

When the wizard looked down, the house lights revealed hawk-like features emphasised by stage make-up. With a thrill of recognition Artie saw that this was indeed the face that had gazed out from hundreds of posters and newspaper photographs: that of Professor John Henry Anderson.

With a graceful gesture the Great Wizard quieted the applause before addressing the crowd.

"Ladies and gentlemen, friends and admirers, welcome to a singular occasion. A few years ago, as many of you will recall, I announced my retirement from the stage. In a long and illustrious career I had achieved all that could be desired – wealth, fame and the admiration of people all over the globe. I decided I had reached that time of life when rest and quiet study would fit me best. But I was wrong."

He paused dramatically and began to walk back and forth across the stage, gesturing with his white-gloved hands, while keeping his gaze fixed intently on his audience.

"One night there came to me in a dream a sort of vision, a tale of magic and mystery and of a great Chinese dragon who swallows a princess. The beautiful maiden miraculously survived to escape its monstrous jaws and fly to freedom. When I awoke I knew, with a certainty as fixed as any religious faith, that I had one more mission in life – to present that very vision to an astonished audience in the crowning illusion of my illustrious career."

Ham breathed in Artie's ear, "Gosh, Artie, do you think that's what we'll see tonight?"

Artie did not reply. He found himself quite mesmerised by the famous magician, who seemed to cast a spell over the entire theatre even without the use of magic.

"My highly trained crew are hard at work refurbishing the long-closed Majestic Theatre to house this new spectacle," Professor Anderson continued, "and there, eight days from today, I shall present to the world the most daring and dangerous magical performance ever attempted: *The Princess and the Dragon!*"

The last words were uttered with such a flourish that the entire audience broke into renewed applause.

The magician thanked them for their enthusiasm then raised a hand for silence.

"I have begun rehearsals for this new extravaganza, but rehearsals are not enough. A magician derives his energy from spectators, and only before the public can he learn if he still has the touch and the talent that made him so famed of old. And so you have been invited here to behold a demonstration of my skills and to see that they have not been dimmed by the passage of years. Among you are leading figures from the world of theatre and entertainment, others of you are acquaintances from my touring days, and some of you are here for reasons unknown even to yourselves."

Artie started at this, wondering if this was a reference to them. He still had no idea why he and Ham had received these exclusive invitations.

"Tonight you shall behold feats both old and new," Anderson announced. "Sleight of hand, conjuring and illusion, all of it in preparation for the new miracle of the stage which I shall unveil in eight days' time at the Majestic Theatre."

With these words he flung up a hand and snatched his top hat out of the empty air. Reaching inside it, he coaxed out a lop-eared white rabbit that blinked around sleepily as if it had been hidden there all through the professor's years of retirement.

From somewhere in the wings a mellow chime rang out like a temple gong. Four assistants, fancifully dressed as oriental monkey gods, filed onto the stage. One of them gathered the rabbit out of the professor's arms and bore it away while the other three went to work setting up an array of tables, screens and cabinets.

And then the magic began in earnest.

The first part of the show involved packs of playing cards. Artie watched spellbound as the Great Wizard of the North executed a breathtaking series of seemingly impossible tricks, producing cards from inside pieces of fruit, passing them invisibly from one hand to the other, then making any card named by a member of the audience pop out of the deck and dance about in the air.

Other amazing feats followed: pulling a string of brightly coloured flags out of a thimble, turning flowers into flame, causing a whole flock of doves to burst from an empty glass bowl.

Next the magician was joined by a handsome young woman in an evening frock of green satin spangled with opalescent sequins. "My daughter Louise remains the most famed mentalist on the planet," he announced. "Once again we shall demonstrate the unique psychic bond that exists between us."

The young woman sat down in a chair and an assistant tied a large silk blindfold over her eyes. Professor

Anderson walked up the aisle through the audience, challenging people to produce objects from their pockets, images of which he would transmit to his daughter by telepathic waves. Each time he gazed at an object and invited Louise to read his thoughts she correctly identified the item, whether it was a watch or a ring or a wallet, and in the case of a wallet she even divined the exact amount of money inside it.

Ham gasped and nudged Artie, who nodded his agreement that this was a baffling demonstration of psychic ability. As the Great Wizard approached their row, Artie noticed the bearded stranger next to him shrink back into his seat, tucking in his chin so that his face was completely overshadowed by his hat.

The magician's bright eyes fixed upon Ham. "I have a notion that this fellow has something rather unusual in his pocket. Is that correct, my young friend?"

Ham was struck dumb and only nodded when Artie gave him a sharp poke.

"Then show us what you have there," the Great Wizard prompted.

Somewhat abashed, Ham reached into his pocket and pulled out a currant bun. There was some good-natured laughter as Anderson said, "Yes, only a schoolboy carries such things in his pocket. And why not? Now, Louise, concentrate on my thoughts. What am I looking at?"

Louise paused then said, "Is it something to eat?"

"It is indeed," said her father. "You are on the right track."

"It's a cake," said the girl confidently. "A currant bun."

"And very delicious, I'm sure," he told Ham with an indulgent smile.

Artie was sure the magician winked at him before he turned and made his way back to the stage accompanied by another round of clapping. Ham slipped the bun back into his pocket. "I thought I might get hungry if the show went on late," he explained sheepishly.

"Do you suppose it's telepathy, or just an ingenious trick?" Artie wondered.

"Either way, it's jolly impressive."

While they were talking in hushed tones, two enormous vases, each large enough to hold a person, were rolled out onto the stage by a pair of assistants. Each vase was painted with exotic images of suns, moons, snakes and swords. A petite girl dressed as an oriental princess skipped lightly onto the stage and took up position between the two great vessels. Gold bracelets decorated her slender arms and a jewelled band encircled her brow.

"And now," the magician announced, "a feat I learned from the mystics of India – the Transposition of the Princess Zafira. Princess, are you prepared for this daring undertaking?"

The princess nodded and, pressing her palms together in front of her, performed a brief but elegant dance to the orchestra's exotic music.

"The tale comes from *The Arabian Nights*," the Great Wizard told the audience, "and tells how Princess Zafira was pursued through the palace by the evil vizier, Nabooz."

Right on cue, the villainous figure of the vizier appeared from behind the left-hand curtain. Beneath his oversized turban a dusky face snarled at the audience with comically exaggerated menace.

"The vizier spotted the princess, who planned to conceal herself inside this enormous vase," said the Great Wizard, pointing to the vessel on the left, "and believed he had her trapped."

The princess wove an agile course around both vases.

"The villain kept his beady eye fixed upon the princess as she performed her dance," the magician narrated. "He was scheming how he would—"

He was interrupted by a squawk from the vizier who was gawking at the left-hand jar, from which a plume of smoke was rising, followed by a spout of flame. Artie assumed this was part of the show until the Great Wizard uttered a gasp of horror and cracks appeared all over the vessel. At the sight of the flames within, the vizier uttered a howl of panic and flung himself headlong into the orchestra pit.

The Great Wizard grabbed the princess and pulled her down beneath him for protection as the giant vase exploded, sending spouts of flame and clay fragments flying in all directions. A cry of alarm went up across the theatre as a streak of fire struck a side curtain and set it ablaze.

Cries broke out from all sides. "Fire! Fire!"

4.

The Joker in the Pack

In the midst of the uproar Artie's eye was caught by the bearded man to his right. Quick as a flash, the stranger leapt from his seat and raced up the aisle towards the exit, his head bowed low to conceal his features beneath the brim of his hat.

Artie was sure that fear of discovery was driving him to flight, not fear of fire. Seizing Ham by the sleeve, he pointed towards the fleeing man. "Quick – we have to stop him!"

Other spectators were now spilling out into the aisle to escape the blaze. With Artie in the lead, the two boys began fighting their way towards the exit.

"Please remain calm!" urged a voice from the stage. "We apologise for this mishap but everything is under control!"

Glancing back, Artie saw some of the stagehands yank

down the burning curtain and hurl buckets of water over it to douse the fire. Others were stamping out smoking embers that were scattered all over the stage.

Artie heard Ham calling out as he struggled to keep up, but there was no time to delay. Taking advantage of his smaller size, he ducked and scrambled his way through the adults until he was darting across the foyer. Bashing through the door out into the street, he spotted the bearded man rounding a corner.

Artie pelted in full pursuit, but by the time he reached the turning, the culprit had vanished, his running footsteps echoing somewhere in the distance. When he paused to catch his breath, Artie noticed something lying on the ground. Bending down, he carefully picked the item up and turned it over in his hands.

It was an oversized playing card, just like the invitations they had all received. On one side was the large question mark, on the other was the grinning face of a joker – an appropriate symbol for someone who seemed to be up to mischief.

Just then Ham caught up and doubled over with his hands on his knees, panting for breath. "Fine thing, leaving me behind like that," he puffed. "Who was that man?"

"I don't know," said Artie with a scowl. "But I'm willing to bet he had something to do with that jar exploding."

Ham straightened up with a sceptical look on his flushed face. "Surely that was just an accident? That chap was no nearer the stage than we were."

"Then why was he so quick to run?"

Ham shrugged. "He might just be a cowardly sort of fellow who takes to his heels at the first hint of danger."

"From the moment he first sat down, it struck me there was something not right about him," Artie insisted. "I'm pretty sure he was wearing a false beard as a disguise. Plus, he dropped this as he was running away." He showed Ham the playing card.

"Well, he's gone now." Ham wiped the sweat from his brow with a handkerchief. "I don't see that there's anything more we can do."

"We have to tell someone." Artie started back towards the theatre. "Perhaps they can use this card to identify him."

All of the audience were out on the street now, setting off for home on foot or by cab. Montague Ruff, who had announced the Great Wizard, was bidding them farewell as they departed.

"Wonderful show, wasn't it? Thank you so much for coming. Only a small mishap. Remember, the Majestic Theatre a week from tomorrow."

By the time Artie and Ham reached him he was heading back inside.

"Wait, sir, wait!" Artie urged as the manager began closing the doors.

The man paused and offered an unsteady smile. "A fine show, eh lads? I'm sure you enjoyed it. No need to make a fuss about a small accident."

"But there was a man with a beard," pressed Artie, displaying the joker card.

"I'm sure there were many bearded men in the audience," the manager responded mildly. "Nothing to be concerned about." With that he shut and locked the doors and disappeared into the theatre.

"He's probably right, you know," said Ham. "It was likely just an accident. Those do happen to magicians. I heard of one who was killed trying to catch a bullet in his teeth."

Artie gazed in frustration at the joker then stuffed the card in his pocket. "It was no accident, Ham. I'm sure of that."

As they headed for home, Ham pulled the bun from his pocket and began munching. "Who invited us, do you think?" he wondered through a mouthful of cake.

Artie's jaw was set firmly. "I don't know, Ham. But I'm determined to find out."

The following afternoon Artie was staring out of his bedroom window at the rain falling on the street outside.

So much for going down to the park to kick a ball around or doing a spot of fishing. With a sigh he turned back to where the three playing cards were laid out on his small desk: the ace of diamonds, the eight of hearts and the joker.

He stared at them intently, willing them to give up their secrets, but they offered him no clue as to what lay behind the events of last night.

If Artie wanted adventure on a rainy day there was just one answer. From the pile of books at his bedside he picked up *Ivanhoe* by Sir Walter Scott, a tale of knights in the time of King Richard the Lionheart. On an impulse, he slipped the three playing cards inside the front cover of the book and headed off to the front room. It had a comfy armchair where he could curl up and read about Ivanhoe's return from the Crusades and his meeting with Robin Hood.

He was crossing the hallway when the front door opened and a soaked figure slouched inside. It was his father, Charles Altamont Doyle, who, when he removed his dripping hat, looked up with a face that was pale and a spirit that was dampened by more than just the weather. Artie was surprised to see his father back so early from his job at the Office of Works, where he dealt with plans for public buildings and street renovations.

"Ah, Artie, a dreich day, is it not?" Even his voice was faint.

"You're home very early today, Father," said Artie,

37

for it was barely three o'clock and his father usually came home from work after six in the evening.

"I was feeling unwell, perhaps a chill," Charles Doyle explained.

Artie's younger sisters, Lottie and Connie, came scampering from their room and rushed to embrace their father. Mr Doyle waved them back good-naturedly.

"Not too close, girls, or you'll get all damp from my coat," he cautioned.

"Papa, listen to this," said Lottie excitedly. She spoke with a slight lisp as she had just lost one of her front milk teeth. "Connie has been learning a poem."

"Yes, and Artie drew me a picture of it," Connie announced, proudly displaying the charcoal sketch of an owl and a cat sitting in a boat.

"Very good, Artie," Charles Doyle complimented his son. "Excellent technique."

"Go ahead, Connie," urged Lottie, "the poem."

Connie pushed her chestnut curls back from her face and recited:

"The Owl and the Pussy-cat went to sea
In a beautiful pea-green boat,
They took some honey, and plenty of money
Wrapped up in a five-pound note."

Mrs Doyle appeared with some sewing in her hand, which she set aside at the sight of her husband. A frown of concern creased her round, pretty face.

"Girls, please," she said, "let your father get out of those wet things. Go back to your needlework."

"Yes, I'll hear the rest of the poem later," said Charles Doyle as the girls skipped back to their room.

"Charles, you're soaked." Mrs Doyle helped him to remove his coat. "You should have taken a carriage home."

"Can't afford that, my love," her husband answered with a wan smile.

Mrs Doyle knew how true this was as she was responsible for the household accounts. Somehow, no matter how little money they had, she always found ways to keep the family well and happy.

"Come," she said cheerfully, "let's get you out of those wet things. I'll make you a hot toddy."

"That would be nice," said Charles Doyle as they disappeared into their bedroom. "I think I may lie down for a while."

Artie gazed around at his father's paintings, which lined the hallway: forest scenes, castles, wild birds in flight. In his imagination and his reading Artie frequently visited the worlds of knights, fairies, dragons and angels that his father brought to life in his paintings. Sadly this was the only place his work was displayed.

His mother appeared from the bedroom looking downcast. As soon as she saw her son, however, she straightened her shoulders and put on a hopeful expression.

"I'm sure your father is going to be fine," she assured him.

"He was in such good spirits when I arrived back from school," Artie recalled.

"Yes, he had such hopes," his mother agreed sadly.

A few weeks ago Charles Doyle had sent samples of his work to a publisher in London, offering to illustrate their forthcoming edition of *The Lives of the Saints*. For weeks he was buoyed up by the hope of being offered the project. However, a letter arrived a week ago explaining that for such a prestigious project they required the services of an established artist.

Mr Doyle was devastated and for days he had shuffled off to work under a cloud of the bleakest melancholy.

"It's so unfair," said Artie, "when his talent is so obvious."

"If he were a bullying, blustering sort of man, and Lord knows there are plenty of those around," said his mother, "he would force his way into the attentions of the art world. But your father is the very soul of human kindness, which makes him the best of men."

With a deep sigh she disappeared into the kitchen

to prepare the hot drink she had promised her husband.

Artie's fingers tightened around the spine of the book he was holding. In the novel all manner of extraordinary events transformed the lives of the characters. He wished that something, anything, would happen to lift the pall of gloom that was hanging over the Doyle household.

As if in answer to his wish, there came a loud rapping at the front door. Artie took a deep breath and opened it, hoping against hope that it wasn't the landlord here to demand the overdue rent. When he saw who was waiting there he almost staggered back in surprise.

There was no mistaking the imposing figure in the black suit and damp rain cape. In his right hand he held a long black cane tipped with silver at both ends, which he had used to knock on the door.

"Excuse me," Professor Anderson asked in a surprisingly mild voice, "but am I addressing Master Arthur Conan Doyle?"

"Y–yes," Artie managed to stammer.

At that moment Mary Doyle appeared and cast an unwelcoming look over the smartly dressed stranger. "Yes, is there something I can do for you?" She used the sharpest of tones, as she always did when meeting someone she suspected was here to demand money.

Artie turned to her and said, "Mama, this is Professor John Henry Anderson – the Great Wizard of the North."

"Indeed I am, madam," the professor acknowledged with a small bow. "And I am here on a matter of great importance that I must discuss with your son."

5.

The Stage Is Set

Mrs Doyle gave her son a curious look then waved the visitor inside. "I suppose you'd better make yourselves comfortable in the sitting room."

She closed the front door as Artie led the magician to the sitting room. Professor Anderson paused to nod admiringly at the paintings on the wall before following. As they settled themselves into the armchairs Mrs Doyle stood in the doorway.

"Can I fetch you a pot of tea, professor?" she offered.

"That would be most kind, madam," said Anderson. He gazed fixedly at her until she took the hint and left, closing the door behind her. He then turned his sharp eyes on Artie.

"Now, young man, what did you make of last night's performance?"

"It was very entertaining…" Artie began, then stopped. "Can I ask you a question, sir?"

43

"Of course, my boy," said the magician affably.

"How did I come to be invited? After all, I've nothing to do with the theatre."

"I saw to it myself that you received a pair of invitations, one for yourself and another for your assistant."

"My assistant?"

"Yes, Mr Humbledon."

"Humbledon? Oh you mean Ham, Mr Hamilton."

"Even so," the professor agreed. "In fact, I had intended to invite you both backstage after the show, but that unhappy incident threw everything into chaos and Montague insisted on locking the place up."

"I still don't understand how you've even heard of us," said Artie.

"You were recommended to me by a mutual acquaintance, Dr William Harthill," the magician explained.

Artie nodded, seeing the connection. Dr Harthill was an experimental doctor who used electricity to cure various ailments. Artie had become friends with him while seeking ways to help his father through his frequent bouts of poor health.

"Some years ago I tried to persuade the good doctor to allow me to incorporate some of his electrical apparatus into my stage performance," Professor Anderson continued. "Though he declined that offer of partnership, we have remained in touch and your name came up in conversation."

"I still don't grasp why you wanted me there."

"Dr Harthill has confided in me about the recent spate of grave robberies, in particular your role in solving the mystery. He assured me that you are both bold and resourceful, just the sort of fellows I need."

"Need? Need for what?" For a moment Artie feared that the professor wanted them for some hazardous stage trick, that they would be shot out of cannons or made targets for a knife-throwing act.

The magician bent forward, leaning on his black cane. "To investigate another mystery." He dropped his voice to a confidential hush. "One which concerns me directly."

Artie found himself leaning closer to the professor and at just this point his mother bustled in with a tea tray. The cups and spoons rattled as she set it down on the table between the two armchairs then proceeded to pour a cup for each of them, adding milk and sugar as requested.

"There's a plate of shortbread here too. Home-baked," Mrs Doyle added proudly. "I do hope you like home baking, professor."

Artie fidgeted at the delay, annoyed that his mother was trying to strike up a conversation with the distinguished visitor. He made a hissing noise to get her attention then inclined his head in the direction of the door. His mother huffed unhappily, but took the hint and left them alone.

"Please go on, sir," Artie urged. He was thoroughly intrigued now and eager to hear more.

"You will recall that last evening ended with a small explosion?" The magician frowned.

Artie nodded.

"What should have happened is this: the princess would have climbed into that vase, then when the vizier peered inside a small bang would have covered his face in soot. The girl would then have leapt out of the other vase, having made a miraculous transference."

"If that had gone off while the vizier was leaning over the vase," said Artie, "he might have been killed."

"Precisely," said the professor grimly. "A much higher concentration of the explosive mixture had been packed into the vase and a shorter fuse placed on it, making the detonation both premature and highly dangerous."

"Could it just have been a mistake?" Artie wondered.

The magician swallowed his tea in one gulp and clapped the cup down decisively. "No, none of my crew are so careless. Someone deliberately sabotaged the trick."

"But why would anyone do that?"

"That is the question," said Professor Anderson. "And it is all the more pressing because this is merely the latest in a series of mishaps which have plagued my rehearsals. Pieces of equipment have turned up broken, costumes have vanished, scenery has collapsed. There have been too many of these incidents for them all to be accidents. No, someone is waging a deliberate campaign of sabotage against me."

"But why?" asked Artie, taking a small slurp of tea. His mother had brewed it so strong it made him wince. She always did this when visitors called, to show them that she had no need to skimp on tea leaves.

"To keep me from returning to the stage." The magician tapped his cane against the table in vexation.

"Who would want to do such a thing?"

Professor Anderson leant back in his chair and spread his arms wide as if to encompass a whole world of suspects. "Who knows? A rival? An old enemy? Or some stranger whose motive cannot even be guessed at?"

"Given that it's become dangerous," said Artie, "isn't it a matter for the police?"

"Oh no, no, no," the professor stated emphatically. "This must be kept private. I cannot afford a scandal or any sort of bad publicity. Queen Victoria will shortly be visiting Edinburgh on her way to Balmoral and I hope for an invitation to perform for her at Holyrood Palace."

"Don't any of the other people in your show have suspicions?" Artie inquired.

The professor shook his head. "To all of my assistants and friends, even to my daughter Louise, I have kept up a front, maintaining that this is merely a series of unconnected accidents. All of my instincts, however, tell me that it is not."

"What can I possibly do to help?" Artie wondered, distractedly taking another sip of tea.

"I need a confidential investigator," said the magician, "someone who can join my crew and never be suspected. My plan is to hire you and Mr Hamilton as stage assistants and in that guise you will seek out the culprit. No one will suppose for a moment that a pair of innocent youngsters could possibly have been hired as detectives."

"And would we be getting… paid for this?" Artie asked hesitantly.

"Of course. There is one week of preparation left before opening night. For that you and your friend would each receive the sum of five shillings."

Artie was turning the possibilities over in his mind. It would mean a break from his summer studies, and even his mother, who was keen that he should keep up with his schoolwork, would surely welcome some extra money coming in. Ham's mother would be even more appreciative of the additional income.

"So we would be employed as stagehands," said Artie.

"On the surface, yes," said the professor. "But beneath the surface you would be investigators. You must, of course, tell no one what your true task is. That must be absolutely confidential."

For a moment Artie recalled how the Trojan hero Aeneas had led his people to safety after the Greeks destroyed their city. Now he not only had an adventure of his own, but the money he earned would help him see his family through their difficulties.

"And what exactly do you want us to look for?" he asked.

"Watch out for any further acts of sabotage. Someone on the inside must be responsible, either from motives of their own or because they have been bribed by some outside party. The presence of an obvious snooper would put them on their guard, but a new pair of assistants will pass unnoticed."

"I may already have a clue," said Artie.

"Indeed?" The magician raised his eyebrows dramatically.

"There was a man seated in my row last night who seemed rather suspicious. He had a thick beard and tinted glasses and kept his hat on throughout the show."

The professor pondered, tapping his cane on the floor as he did so. "Black beard, tinted glasses... It certainly sounds like a disguise. What else did he do to arouse your suspicions?"

"Well, when the explosion came, he immediately jumped from his seat and ran outside. I chased him but couldn't catch up. He did drop something though."

Artie opened his book and took out the card he had found lying on the ground. "If you don't mind my asking, how were the words on the back replaced by a question mark?"

"A trifle," the professor responded with a dismissive wave of his hand. "The question mark was printed there all along but painted over with a chemical coating and special ink which evaporate after a few minutes of contact with the air."

"Right…" Artie mused on how simple it sounded when it was explained.

When the magician turned over the card and saw the joker's face grinning at him his eyes grew wide. "This is most disturbing," he breathed.

"I suspected as much," Artie said gravely.

"What puzzles me," said the magician darkly, "is that we did not use jokers for the invitations. This is the card of an intruder."

He flipped the card over between his fingers then slipped it into his pocket. "Report to the Majestic Theatre on Jeffrey Street tomorrow morning at eight o'clock, Mr Doyle," he instructed. "You and your assistant. Perhaps between us we can get to the bottom of this."

Artie followed the professor into the hallway where, in answer to his knock, Mrs Doyle was just letting Ham inside. The magician tipped his hat politely to both of them then slipped out.

Ham gaped. "Artie, do you know who that was?"

"Of course I know," said Artie, leading his friend into the front room, away from the prying eyes of his suspicious mother. "It was Professor Anderson, the Great Wizard of the North. I've just been having tea with him."

"What?" Ham was aghast. "But this is simply amazing! What on earth does he want with you, Artie?"

"He wants to hire us – both of us – as stagehands for his show. We'll be working for him for the next week or so."

"Well, that's splendid news. But why us? What do we know about being stagehands?"

"That's just a cover story, Ham," Artie explained. "He actually wants us to investigate a series of accidents that have plagued his show. That explosion last night was just the latest."

"You mean," said Ham excitedly, "that we're being hired as... as..."

"Yes, Ham, as detectives."

"Why, that's marvellous!"

"Look, Ham," said Artie, thinking of what had almost happened to the vizier, "before you agree to doing this, you need to be aware that it could be dangerous."

Ham's smile drooped for an instant, then his eye drifted to the tea tray. "In that case, could I have a piece of shortbread?"

6.

The Theatrical Phenomenon

Next morning, as Artie arrived at Ham's home in Buccleugh Street, he first had to push his way past his friend's huge black dog Berrybus, who insisted on greeting everyone who came through the door by washing their face with his big tongue. Ham was in the kitchen about to start on his second boiled egg.

"Can't a fellow finish his breakfast in peace?" he complained as Artie dragged him from the table.

"Not when there's work to be done." Artie helped him on with his jacket.

"Eddie, don't you dare leave without your lunch," said his mother, pressing a small paper-wrapped bundle into his hands.

Mrs Hamilton was surprisingly thin for a woman who did so much baking, and her spectacles made her eyes look huge and anxious.

"Don't fret, Mother," Ham assured her as Artie bustled him to the door. "I promise not to go hungry."

Berrybus tried to follow them outside and it took a lot of heaving and grunting from both boys to shove the huge mastiff back inside.

"Stay put, there's a good chap," puffed Ham, giving the dog a last bite of toast. "I'll see you later."

"We don't want to be late to our first case," said Artie as they walked down the road. "What would the client think?"

"I certainly wouldn't want a magician cross with me," Ham conceded. "He would probably have all sorts of ways of getting back at you. You might wake up to find your bed full of frogs, or on top of a mountain or something worse."

The Majestic Theatre was much larger than the Pantheon, built of granite and marble with a frieze of the Nine Muses running above the doorway. A doorman in a maroon uniform with gold braid on his shoulders and cap barred their way. When Artie explained who they were the doorman waved them inside.

"Mind your step," he warned. "There's planks and ladders lying all over the place."

The foyer was bare except for a few benches and a rolled-up carpet. From the open doors beyond came the smell of fresh paint and the busy din of hammering and sawing. When they passed through into the auditorium it looked more like a workshop than a theatre.

Men in coveralls were standing on ladders fixing gold masks to the walls. Others were busily erecting scaffolding or working on the stage itself. Voices shouted out instructions from the balcony high overhead.

Artie recognised the professor's daughter Louise Anderson making her way towards them through the bustle. In contrast to her stage attire, she was dressed in a plain brown skirt and tailored blouse, her long black hair bound up in a bun. She greeted them with a friendly smile.

"Ah, the boy with the cake!"

"How did you know that?" gasped Ham. "I mean, not how did you know this is me now, but how did you know about the cake when you were doing your mind-reading act? Though come to think of it, how do you know me now? You were blindfolded that night so how would you... Hang on, I'm starting to confuse myself."

Louise laughed pleasantly. "I can't go giving away my secrets now, can I? My father says he's hired you two to assist us because you come highly recommended."

Artie wondered if Louise suspected their real mission.

54

"We'll do our best not to let you down," he responded neutrally.

He recognised the portly figure of Montague Ruff hurrying towards them.

"Oh there you are, Miss Louise!" the theatrical manager exclaimed. "I need you to go over your lighting cues with young Alec." He rolled his eyes. "It will be a miracle if that boy doesn't plunge the whole theatre into darkness."

"Don't fret yourself, Mr Ruff." Louise patted his arm. "Everything will be fine. In fact, Father has just hired some additional help." She introduced the boys to Ruff just before he scampered off on some further piece of business. Other introductions quickly followed. Artie found himself shaking hands with Laurence Galbraith, a small, sandy-haired man in a paint-spotted cap and coveralls, whom he recognised at second glance as the evil vizier from the ill-fated Pantheon performance.

"Laurence has been Father's assistant for years," said Louise, "and is responsible for many of the mechanical devices behind his most stunning illusions."

Galbraith was just heading off, hammer in hand, when he suddenly gasped, "Oh, I say!"

He was looking up towards the roof. Following his gaze, Artie saw a slight female figure in a leotard descending a rope in a series of lithe twists. As she alighted daintily on the floor, Louise beckoned Artie and Ham forward.

"This is Mademoiselle Delphine," she informed them. "You may recognise her as Princess Zafira from the other night."

Delphine looked to be about twenty, but she was so petite she could easily be taken for someone much younger. Ham appeared quite struck by the girl's elfin beauty.

"I'm very pleased, very, very pleased to meet you, mademoiselle," he gabbled, "very pleased indeed."

Delphine murmured a few words of greeting in a soft, French-accented voice, then returned to her rehearsals.

Louise took the boys behind the stage and handed them over to Fergus Donnelly, a lanky Irishman who was in charge of the work crew. He led the boys on a brief tour of the theatre, stepping over ropes and ducking around sandbags that were hanging from the ceiling.

"I'm glad you lads have showed up," he said. "We're a bit short-handed on account of so many folk leaving."

"Leaving?" said Artie. "Why?"

"Well, there have been a few accidents and, theatre folk being a superstitious lot – I mean you only have to mention the Scottish play to send them diving for cover – well, some of them took fright like there's something spooky about this place."

"Spooky?" groaned Ham. "I don't like the sound of that."

"Why should they think that?" asked Artie.

"The reason the Majestic's been closed up so long," said Fergus, "is that there was a fire here a few years ago and about half a dozen people were killed. Before we moved in to restore it, some of the locals claimed they saw weird lights and shadowy figures moving about the place."

"Shadowy figures?" Ham looked nervously about him.

"Right," said Fergus. "There's some as think the ghosts of the dead still haunt the place, like unhappy customers demanding their money back."

"Do you believe that?" asked Artie.

"Havers!" Fergus scoffed. "If every spot where somebody died was haunted, you couldn't move for ghosts. It's just a streak of bad luck is all. And as every gambler knows, a bad streak, like a good one, eventually runs out and things go back to normal."

Artie and Ham were soon set to work fetching and carrying, sweeping up sawdust, and brewing pots of tea for the workmen. They had just finished polishing some brasswork at the front of the stage when a red-haired girl made a flamboyant entrance from the back of the theatre.

She sailed up the aisle towards the stage, head proudly erect, like a queen acknowledging the applause of an invisible, adoring audience. Her blue dress was elaborately flounced, its frills accentuating her sweeping movements. Draped around her shoulders was a shawl of silver-edged lace that billowed behind her like butterfly wings.

The boys stood and stared as she halted directly in front of them. She was a few inches taller than Artie and had large brown eyes that surveyed them with frank curiosity.

"Aren't you going to introduce yourselves?" she asked primly. "Or have you no manners where you come from?"

Artie bristled at being addressed in so haughty a manner by a girl who couldn't be much older than himself.

"We come from Edinburgh," he retorted. "I'm Arthur Conan Doyle – Artie."

"And I'm Edward Hamilton," said Ham. "Ha— er... Edward."

"Oh, those names won't do at all," the girl tutted. "In the theatre we must have romantic names." She pressed a finger to the tip of her chin to make it clear that she was pondering the problem. "I know," she declared, pointing to them each in turn, "you shall be Arturo and you shall be Eduardo. Yes, that's it, Arturo and Eduardo."

"But we're not Italian," Artie objected.

"No, I'm afraid you're not, Arturo," said the girl pityingly. "But Italian names are so colourful, perhaps some of that will rub off on you."

"I don't want anything rubbing off on me," Ham declared stubbornly.

"Look, who are you anyway?" Artie struggled to remain polite.

The girl tossed her head, sending her copper curls bouncing. "I am Miss Rowena McCleary," she announced grandly. She paused and peered down her nose at the two boys, as if doubting their command of the English language. "You've heard of me, of course."

"No," said Ham bluntly, "we haven't."

"Well, *you will*," the girl asserted confidently. "I am already widely referred to as the Theatrical Phenomenon."

"Referred to by whom?" Artie inquired sceptically.

"People of course," the girl asserted, "people everywhere. Because of my breathtaking range of talents."

"What sort of talents are they exactly?" asked Ham.

"To begin with, there's acting, of course," said the girl. She struck a tragic pose, one hand clasped to her chest, the other pressed to her forehead. "Then there's singing – everything from light opera to lieder –" she paused to emit a piercing soprano note, "and, of course, dancing."

She performed an elaborate pirouette and finished facing the boys with a beaming smile, as though she expected them to clap.

"She says 'of course' an awful lot, doesn't she?" Ham muttered aside to Artie.

Looking slightly miffed at their lack of response, Rowena McCleary folded her arms and arched an eyebrow. "And what are the pair of you? Are you acrobats? Jugglers? Comedians perhaps?"

"We're here to help out in all sorts of ways," said Ham.

"We have a pretty breathtaking range of talents ourselves," said Artie.

The Phenomenon eyed him coldly. "Such as?"

"Oh, painting scenery, handling props," Artie replied.

"Adjusting the lighting," Ham added.

"Oh, stage crew." Rowena was unimpressed. "If you ask me, you'd be better as comedians. You'd at least entertain people who enjoy the crude, clodhopping sort of humour. Every show has room for a couple of buffoons."

Ham flushed indignantly. "I'll have you know we're here on a very important assignment."

"Really?" said the girl, her interest suddenly piqued. "What sort of an assignment?"

"To make the tea," Artie interjected.

He seized Ham by the arm and dragged him away. "You're not going to make much of a detective if you start blabbing about our real job as soon as you get here," he chided.

"Sorry, Artie," Ham apologised, abashed. "It's just that girl's rather annoying and I let her provoke me."

"She's just a theatre person," Artie told him soothingly.

"I think they're all a bit full of themselves. You'd have to be to get up on stage in front of hundreds of strangers night after night."

"I suppose so. I hope they're not all as bad as she is."

They went backstage, looking for a kettle to boil some water. They were passing an open doorway when they heard a groan of anguish come from the room beyond. Peering in they saw Professor Anderson seated at an untidy desk surrounded by trunks and papers. As soon as he spotted them he waved them urgently inside.

"My young friends," he moaned, "I'm afraid something terrible has happened."

7.

Mad as a Hatter

Artie's mind started racing through a whole series of possible tragedies that could have befallen the professor. "There hasn't been another fire, has there?"

Ham glanced uneasily upwards. "I hope the roof isn't collapsing."

"No, no, it's nothing like that," said the magician. "It's Fernando – Fernando McTavish, my set designer."

"What's happened to him?" Artie wondered if the man had fallen victim to another act of sabotage.

"Has he been kidnapped?" asked Ham.

"Worse," sighed the magician. "He's run off to Italy to marry a contessa. What am I to do now? Where will I find an artist to complete the job at such short notice? We only have backdrops for half the scenes."

Artie pricked up his ears. "You need an artist?"

The magician nodded glumly.

"I think I can recommend someone," Artie offered eagerly. "You've already seen some of his work in my home."

"Those paintings in the hallway?"

"Yes, they were painted by my father."

The professor's face brightened hopefully. "Would he be available to begin work at once?"

"I think he could be," said Artie.

That night Professor Anderson went home with Artie. They found Charles Doyle seated at the kitchen table about to pour himself a glass of wine. As soon as Artie explained the reason for the professor's visit, his father placed the cork back in the bottle and set the glass aside. He fetched his sketchpad and, as the magician explained his requirements, rapidly produced some rough drawings of mountains, the interior of a Chinese palace and an enchanted woodland.

"These are excellent," the professor approved. "You've grasped the concept admirably."

There followed a brief discussion of terms of payment, deadlines and an assurance that the name of Charles Altamont Doyle would feature in the programme accompanying the magic show.

As soon as the Great Wizard had left, Mr Doyle hopped delightedly around the room.

"Artie my boy, this is the beginning of great things

for us!" he exclaimed. "What a stroke of fortune! What a lucky chance you were hired to work at that theatre!"

At this point Mrs Doyle returned from visiting a recently widowed friend. She gasped in amazement as her husband seized her in an affectionate hug, and the excitement brought their two small daughters scampering in.

"Charles, whatever has come over you?"

In a stream of excited babble Charles Doyle explained what had happened.

"But, Charles," she objected anxiously, "however will you find the time? You cannot take any more days off and still retain your position at the Office of Works."

"Never fear," Charles Doyle assured her confidently. "I have evenings and lunchtimes and an entire weekend ahead. And I shall be operating in the white heat of pure inspiration."

"Well, Charles, in that case, this is happy news," his wife beamed.

"Indeed, we need to celebrate!" Mr Doyle declared. "Do you know what I'm going to do?"

Artie couldn't help casting an anxious glance at the wine bottle, but his father was pointing at the stove.

"I'm going to make some French toast!" he announced triumphantly.

Next day, the boys were kept busy with all manner of odd jobs around the theatre. They soon became used to the clatter of hammers and boards, the dusty air and the smell of paint and turpentine. While they carried out their duties they kept an eye on everyone, looking for some clue as to who might be causing the accidents. Now and again they would pick up a snatch of conversation or overhear a complaint about the working conditions, but nothing to indicate who the culprit might be.

During a break they found a quiet corner behind the stage where they could drink some lemonade and discuss their progress – or lack of it. Artie got out his notebook and made a list of suspects.

The Case of the Theatre Sabotage

List of potential suspects:

- Laurence Galbraith, the professor's assistant
- Montague Ruff, theatrical manager
- Miss Louise Anderson, the professor's daughter
- Fergus Donnelly, the works foreman
- Mademoiselle Delphine, dancer
- Wilkie, the doorman
- The mysterious bearded 'Joker' – who is he?

"The trouble is," said Artie, "that you end up looking for villainy everywhere. Like when that chap slipped off the ladder this morning."

"Pick a card, Artie."

Artie looked up and saw Ham was holding out a deck of playing cards spread out face down. "What?"

"I said pick a card," Ham repeated. "Look, I thought that now we're part of a magic show, we should get into the spirit of it, so I picked up a book of card tricks and I've been practising them at home."

"I am trying to concentrate on the case," Artie objected.

"This will help," Ham insisted. "It will get you inside the mind of a magician."

With a sigh, Artie pulled out a card at random and looked at it. It was the ten of spades.

"Now, without letting me see it, slide it back into the deck," Ham instructed.

He complied and Ham shuffled the cards energetically.

"I examined the ladder," said Artie, resuming his earlier thought, "but I couldn't tell if it had been tampered with."

Ham flicked through the cards and held one out triumphantly. "And this," he declared, "is your card!" It was the three of diamonds.

"No, it isn't," said Artie. "The trouble is, you see, with all the work going on around here, there are bound to be some genuine accidents."

Frowning at the cards, Ham selected another one and displayed it defiantly. "Right then, this is definitely your card." It was the queen of spades.

"No, it's not," said Artie. "So the problem is how to separate the genuine accidents from acts of sabotage."

"Artie, are you absolutely sure this isn't your card?" Ham was almost pleading.

"Quite sure."

"I don't understand it," Ham scowled. "I'm sure I followed the instructions to the letter." With an unhappy grunt he stuffed the cards back into his pocket and took a swig of lemonade.

"Look," Artie showed Ham his notebook, "here's my list of suspects."

Ham peered at the list. "Well, if we're looking for a culprit," he said darkly, "I vote for that awful girl."

Artie blinked. "Rowena? Why would she want to sabotage the show?"

"For revenge," said Ham. "Haven't you seen her pestering the professor and his daughter, asking for a bigger part? She thinks she should be playing the princess instead of Delphine. I'll bet if they won't let her be the star she's going to scupper the whole thing."

"But then she wouldn't get to be on stage at all," Artie pointed out.

"That won't matter to her," said Ham. "She's mad as a hatter."

Artie shrugged and added to his list:

The mysterious bearded joker – who is he?

• Miss Rowena McCleary, the T.P.

As shocking as a lightning flash, the Theatrical Phenomenon suddenly bounded from behind a curtain and thrust herself between the two boys.

"What are you two muttering about now?" she demanded. "I swear there are times you act more like spies than stagehands."

Artie hastily snapped his notebook shut and stuffed it in his pocket.

"We were just talking about our school work," he said.

"Yes, don't *you* have any studying to do?" Ham asked pointedly.

"The Montecelli College for Young Gentlewomen in Switzerland is a very exclusive school," Rowena informed them haughtily, "employing the latest scientific methods of education. During term time they inculcate sufficient knowledge that during the summer months we are advised to leave off studying and broaden our experience of life. Which is exactly what I'm doing here."

"You won't broaden it much by hanging around bothering us," said Ham.

For a moment there was a flicker of hurt in the girl's bright eyes, but she quickly recovered her poise. "I feel it enlarges the soul to talk with people from every walk of life," she asserted proudly, "no matter how low their station."

As the only other young person involved in the show, Artie didn't want to bicker with Rowena. He tried to think of a way to improve relations.

"I'm sure it's very kind of you to take an interest," he said pleasantly. "Would you like some lemonade?"

He offered her the bottle. Rowena wrinkled her nose fastidiously.

"You don't have a glass I could use, do you?" she inquired politely.

"We couldn't find any," said Ham. "It's quite safe to drink from the bottle. We're not diseased or anything."

Rowena shook her head. "I have some bottled Alpine water in my dressing room. That will be better for preserving my voice. But thank you for your offer. I'd better go and rehearse my song now."

She backed away and disappeared, singing to herself:

"An exile from home splendour dazzles in vain,
Oh give me my lowly thatched cottage again..."

"She's been rehearsing that song every day," said Artie as the girl's voice faded into the distance.

"And it still sounds like rubbish," said Ham. "What is she doing here anyway? Why on earth is the professor letting her be part of the show?"

"I heard somebody say it's because her father is helping to finance the refurbishment of the theatre."

"Oh well, that it explains it," said Ham. "She's not nearly as talented as she thinks she is."

"Nobody is that talented," Artie agreed.

They went back to work, cleaning the rows of seats, which had been left unoccupied for years. The cleaning materials had a pungent smell and they had to take frequent breaks to avoid choking.

On the stage Professor Anderson was supervising the positioning of certain props, such as fake palm trees and oriental screens. Off to one side a pianist was running through his repertoire of tunes.

"You know, Artie..." Ham blew his nose to clear his head of the fumes. "I think we should take a different tack on this. Suppose the theatre is cursed?"

"Ham, if there was a curse on this theatre, why would the vase have exploded on a completely different stage?"

70

"Alright then," said Ham, "maybe somebody put a curse on the professor. You know, like a witch who's jealous of his powers."

"So you're saying we should look for a witch," Artie pressed sceptically. "How would we go about that?"

"I don't know. Don't they all gather at a crossroads at midnight to commune with their cats or something? Still, even if we did track down a witch, I don't know how we'd go about lifting a curse."

"Ham, I'm quite sure there are no witches involved in this case," Artie assured him.

"Oh really?" Ham's eyes grew wide. "What about her?"

He was pointing at a fearsome woman who was striding down the aisle towards them with an angry expression on her face. Her eyes blazed with a manic energy that was both terrifying and mesmerising.

Artie felt a cold chill run through his bones. Perhaps Ham was right after all. If there were such things as witches, this was surely their queen.

8.

Madame Sophonisba

The figure stalking towards them was the most extraordinary person Artie had ever beheld. She was a woman of medium height, but wore a towering headdress bedecked with jewels and feathers that made her seem twice as tall. Her voluminous purple robe was lavishly embroidered with the signs of the zodiac picked out in black, silver and gold. She paused in the middle of the theatre and gestured at her surroundings with an imperious sweep of her arm.

"Take warning, all of you here!" she cried out in a voice like a screeching winter gale. "As you value your lives, flee this place before it is too late!"

The various workmen nearby, all of whom looked tough enough to handle themselves, cowered away from her as though her breath might scorch their skin.

The woman had two companions. One was a small,

nervous lady who bobbed in and out of sight behind her like a bird hopping about in a cage. The other was a man in a green frock coat with a red face and huge white side-whiskers. He nodded emphatically in support of every word the woman in the purple robe spoke.

"There is a curse upon this place," she continued in the same ear-piercing tone, "and upon you, Professor John Henry Anderson, upon you most of all!"

She stood straight and gaunt, like an accusing judge, and glared ominously at the professor.

"Madam," said Anderson stiffly, "I must ask you to leave here at once. You are interfering in my legitimate business."

"As you interfere in mine!" the woman retorted. She snatched a newspaper her bird-like companion was holding and shook it angrily at Anderson. "You gave an interview to the press denouncing those who, you suggest, use trickery and illusion to claim they have supernatural powers."

"Swindling money from innocent people with false prophecies of the future is immoral," said the magician. "I have no reason to believe you have changed your ways."

The woman hurled the paper to the floor ahead of her and trampled over it as she advanced towards the stage with her two followers in tow. The boys retreated up the steps onto the stage. To their relief, however, the ferocious woman's attention was focused not on them but on Professor Anderson.

"You are the faker," she intoned darkly, "pitting your pathetic trickery against those who wield true power."

All around, the theatre workers and performers stood aghast, struck dumb by the sheer force of the woman's blazing malice.

Louise appeared from the wings to join the boys at the side of the stage. She glowered at the self-proclaimed prophetess with steely dislike.

"Who on earth is this person?" Artie asked her in an urgent whisper.

"She calls herself Madame Sophonisba," Louise replied. "If my father has one true enemy in all the world, it is that woman."

Madame Sophonisba's attention was fixed rigidly on the professor. "My powers are the gift of the great goddess Astarte," she proclaimed shrilly, "and the wonders I have performed are the proof of them."

The bird-like woman beside her piped, "Oh yes, yes!"

"Tricks and illusions," said Professor Anderson. "You have been found out before and you will be exposed again."

"Take heed, sir, take heed," warned the white-haired man, his face flushing to an even deeper shade of crimson. "This lady is gifted with the most remarkable abilities. The past and the future alike lie open to her vision and you would be wise not to cross her."

Madame Sophonisba pointed an accusing finger.

"I see your future all too clearly, Anderson. You will bring ruin upon yourself and everyone about you unless you abandon this foolish and prideful enterprise. The spirits will not abide to see you performing your childish nonsense in this place of death. Go back home and use your tricks to amuse your grandchildren."

She turned on her heel and retraced her steps, her two admirers trailing after.

"Your threats are as empty as your ridiculous claims of power," Anderson called after her. "I warn you not to bother me again."

Madame Sophonisba paused and looked back.

"You warn me? You fool!" She waved her arms about her. "You mark my words, Anderson. If you persist in your folly, all of this will end in fire!"

With those awful words she stalked out of the theatre.

Artie could see that the professor was struggling to maintain his dignity.

"Alright everyone, back to work," he ordered as he headed backstage. "Pay no attention to the ravings of that madwoman."

Ham's back was still pressed flat against a pillar at the side of the stage. "Whether or not she has magic powers," he gasped, "she is rather scary."

Louise made a derisive noise. "That's her only real talent. Everything else she does is for effect."

"You've had trouble with her before," Artie observed.

Louise's eyes were still smouldering with anger. "A few years ago she convinced a number of wealthy people that she was receiving messages from this goddess Astarte she talks about, messages that gave her an insight into the future. She backed up her claims with a few simple illusions – walking through walls, conjuring music out of thin air. My father recreated all of her feats in public to demonstrate there were no supernatural powers at work. The woman was disgraced and had to leave town to escape the scandal. Now she is back and trying to rebuild her tattered reputation with a new bag of tricks."

She gave herself a shake to regain her composure. "She's a blusterer, nothing more. Now excuse me, I have to talk to the seamstress about the costumes for the final part of the show."

Left alone, the boys looked at each other.

"It sounds like this Madame Soapdish has a grudge against the professor," Ham remarked.

"If she's sabotaging his show," said Artie, "it would be a bit foolish to storm in here like that and make herself an obvious suspect."

"Who knows?" said Ham. "I'm beginning to think we're the only people here who aren't crackpots. And sometimes I'm not sure about you."

Artie sought out the professor in his office and found him seated at his desk drinking a glass of milk of magnesia.

"I'm afraid that wild lady has upset my stomach," the magician explained. "I find any talk of fire upsetting."

"Yes, of course," said Artie. "How did you two cross paths?"

"An acquaintance of mine had given her a considerable sum of money," Professor Anderson recalled, "in exchange for her assurance that the goddess Astarte would rain blessings down upon him. I decided to investigate and arranged to be present at a demonstration of her powers."

"What happened?" asked Artie.

The professor laughed. "She was tied to a chair with ropes while a trumpet and a drum were laid at her feet. She was then surrounded by a screen so she could not be seen, with observers placed on every side to guarantee that no one could enter or leave the enclosed area. Then, amazingly, the instruments began to play. When the music stopped, the screen was pulled away and there sat Madame Sophonisba, bound as tightly as before and completely unable to move from the chair."

"That does sound quite impressive," Artie felt forced to admit.

"Child's play!" scoffed the professor. He opened one of his desk drawers and brought out a length of rope. "Do you know how to tie a good knot, my boy?"

"I learned a few when they took us boating at school," said Artie.

"Good. Now I'll place my hands behind the back of the chair and you tie me as tightly as you can."

"If you insist, sir," said Artie.

When he was finished he faced the professor with a smile of satisfaction. "There, sir. I think you'll find that…"

The words froze in his mouth as the professor immediately stood up, his arms free and the loose rope dangling from one hand.

"But how…?" Artie gasped.

"Escaping from a knotted rope is the simplest thing in the world, once you know how it's done." The magician beckoned him closer. "Here, let me teach you."

By the time he rejoined Ham, Artie was feeling quite pleased with how quickly he had mastered the professor's rope escape techniques. He found his friend sitting on a box at the side of the stage watching Delphine rehearse one of her dances to the pianist's accompaniment. The French girl moved with fairy-like lightness, her diaphanous costume swirling about her.

"She's very wonderful, isn't she?" Ham sighed. "She was telling me that she's an orphan. When her mother died in Paris last year, she decided to come to Scotland to start a new life here."

"I've been with the professor," said Artie, "getting some more information about Madame Sophonisba."

A long cord dangled from the rafters above and at the climax of her performance, Delphine leapt up and caught hold of it. With one slender arm extended before her and a leg stretched out behind, she swung back and forth across the stage as though she were flying.

All around, members of the crew were watching in rapt admiration. Ham was so delighted he started clapping. The mood changed dramatically, however, when, without warning, the cord snapped and Delphine came tumbling down out of the air.

There were cries of shock all around as the young woman hit the stage hard and rolled over three times with a squeal of pain. Everyone rushed to assist her, but it was Ham who helped her to her feet.

"Delphine, are you alright?" he gasped.

"*Oui, ce n'est rien.*" The girl rubbed her arm. "I have bruised my elbow, that is all."

"Maybe you should lie down," Artie suggested.

Delphine gave a small shake of her head. "We have only a few days left to rehearse. We cannot waste the time."

The professor had come running onto the stage, drawn by the sounds of alarm. He rushed to Delphine's side to assure himself that she was not seriously injured.

Artie noticed that Louise had picked up the broken cord and was examining it. He joined her and saw the grim tightness of her lips.

"It looks to me as though the cord has been partly cut," she said.

"Who could have done that?" asked Artie.

Louise's brow creased. "It was thoroughly examined just before Delphine came on stage. I don't see how anyone could have interfered with it."

Professor Anderson had overheard their conversation and he drew Artie and Ham urgently aside.

"The mischief continues," he growled. "And there may be worse to come."

"How do you mean, sir?" asked Artie.

"I think," the professor responded gravely, "it is time I took you to meet the dragon."

9.

The Dragon Entertains

As they followed the professor outside, Ham leaned close to Artie and muttered, "Artie it's obvious who caused that accident to Delphine. That girl, the Whatsit Phenomenon, wants to injure her so she can take her place."

Artie signalled to his friend to keep his voice down so that Professor Anderson wouldn't overhear. "Even if it was Rowena," he murmured, "how could she possibly have interfered with the cord? You heard Louise say it had been checked beforehand."

Ham made a sour face and shrugged.

Out in the street the professor hailed a horse-drawn cab and the three of them travelled across town to Leith. Here they disembarked, and the magician sent the cabbie off with a handsome tip.

"What are we doing here?" Ham wondered. "I can't see anything but factories and warehouses."

"Follow me!" The professor set off down a side street. "I've kept the location secret for a very good reason."

They followed him to a large brick building with a set of double doors. Professor Anderson pointed to three sturdy locks.

"I have the only set of keys," he said. "Every morning I open the place up so my engineers can get in and last thing at night I come back to lock the doors securely." He drew a ring of keys from his pocket and jingled them. "No one can get in here without these."

He opened one of the doors and ushered the boys inside before following himself. There was a metallic tang in the air mixed with the smell of oil and grease. Artie's vision took a moment to adjust from the summer sunshine outside to the relatively dim light provided by some oil lanterns and a small barred window set high in the far wall.

A gigantic shape occupied the centre of the warehouse and the sight of it made Artie's eyes almost pop out.

Ham stared in astonishment. "Artie, d–do you see it?"

"Yes, I do," said Artie. "It's a dragon!"

The monster was the size of an elephant and covered in scales of shimmering green. Two thin tendrils of white smoke drifted from its nostrils and its eyes glowed bright red like a pair of burning coals. It squatted upon four sets of claws that looked like they could slash their way through a brick wall and its magnificent wings, decorated with veins of shining crimson, spread out from its back like elegant sails.

Two men in coveralls stood close by the monster, neither showing any concern for his own safety.

"Ah, Professor Anderson, sir," greeted the taller one, "you're just in time."

"That's right," the shorter man agreed. "We were about to run Oswald through his paces."

"Who's Oswald?" Artie managed to ask, though his mouth had gone completely dry.

"That's the name Mr Wharton and Mr Low here have given to my dragon," said the professor. "I can't think where they got it from."

"It just seems appropriate somehow," said Mr Wharton, the tall man, patting the dragon's neck as if it were a prize racehorse.

"Come on then, Oswald, show us your stuff," prompted Mr Low.

They stepped away and immediately there came the noise of gears grating and shifting inside the monster. With a metallic creak the wings slowly rose and the huge head turned towards the newcomers, fixing its blazing eyes upon them.

Ham instinctively took a step back.

"It's alright," Artie told him. "It's just a machine."

"That is correct," Professor Anderson confirmed, "a magnificent machine."

The dragon's jaws cranked open to emit a thunderous roar accompanied by a gust of pitchy vapour.

"Smells like he ate something horrible for his breakfast," said Ham, waving a hand under his nose.

"It sounds like it too," said Artie as something rumbled in the dragon's innards.

Even though he knew it was a machine, he still couldn't keep from trembling at the sheer, vast might of the thing. When it raised a ferocious claw and made a vicious rip at the empty air, it was all he could do not to scamper for the door.

"I'm sure he's quite tame." Ham grinned nervously. "He surely doesn't want to hurt anyone."

"Of course not," said Professor Anderson. "He was created to entertain, nothing more than that."

"So this is to be the centrepiece of your new show?" asked Artie as the dragon's wings and head continued to move in an impressive display of animation.

"Indeed!" the magician enthused. "Imagine the scene upon the stage, lads, as we act out the legendary tale from ancient China. I shall narrate thus:

"It was in the village of Po-Shai that all the people lived in terror of the mighty dragon Fenfang. The only way to set him at peace and keep him from destroying their homes and their lives

was to send each year a single maiden to be devoured by him."

As if on cue the dragon raised its great head and gave a hungry growl, its sharp, metallic teeth flashing.

"He does seem peckish," Ham observed anxiously.

"*This year, oh the tragedy!*" Professor Anderson walked around the dragon as he spoke, making dramatic gestures with his hands. "*The beloved Princess Kiki has been selected by lot as the sacrifice. She has no wish to be devoured, but what is she to do? She must pay the price for the safety of her people. But as luck would have it, there happened into the valley at this time the great wizard Azubar* – played, of course, by yours truly."

The professor paused to take a small bow before continuing.

"*The wizard swore that he would cast a spell upon the beautiful princess that would protect her against all harm. And so the fateful day came when the princess entered the lair of the dragon, while from a hiding place close by, the wizard prepared his enchantments.*"

There came a rumble from the dragon's throat, then a ball of fire tumbled from his jaws and rolled down his great chest to burst into smoke and ash on the stone floor.

"Artie, if we had been standing even a little closer…" Ham gasped.

"Yes, I know," said Artie with a gulp. "Best not to think about it."

He noticed that the two engineers were standing well

to one side and nodding approvingly as they watched their wonderful construction perform.

"*As the princess entered the dragon's lair,*" Professor Anderson intoned grandly, "*the wizard cast his spell. Behold!* The light grows dim as the terrible jaws close upon the princess, and they are both enveloped in a cloud of white smoke. Suddenly, there is the dragon, flying over the heads of the theatre audience upon his outspread wings."

He stared upwards as if imagining the awesome sight, then thrust out an arm. "The wizard flings a handful of enchanted powder and the dragon is consumed in a blast of fire. As everyone gasps in astonishment, out of the smoke and ash, the princess descends into their midst unharmed. There follows lengthy and sustained applause which shakes the very walls!"

Once again the magician bowed and Artie and Ham found themselves clapping enthusiastically, as though they had actually witnessed the astounding events he had described.

The dragon had ceased its mechanical movements and now, to the boys' surprise, a door clanked open in its belly. Laurence Galbraith, the professor's assistant, clambered out, wiping the sweat from his face with a rag.

"It's very hot inside there, sir," he panted. "We'll need a supply of iced water if I'm to make it to the end of the trick."

The magician put an arm around the smaller man and patted his shoulder. "Larry, you shall have every comfort we can provide," he promised. "And may I compliment you on a magnificent performance."

While the Great Wizard and his assistants continued to enthuse with each other, Artie and Ham digested this new development.

"So that's how it comes alive," said Ham. "There's a man inside working the controls."

"I can't help thinking of the fire that thing was belching up," said Artie apprehensively. "Remember what happened with the exploding vase?"

Ham's eyes widened. "Oh, Artie, what will happen if the dragon should blow up in the middle of a performance?"

"It would be a disaster," said Artie, "a complete and deadly disaster. It would probably destroy the entire theatre."

The two boys stared at each other, suddenly aware that it was up to them to prevent such a calamity.

10.

The Disappearing Pharaoh

The next morning Artie still felt the weight of responsibility upon him as he and Ham walked down to the theatre. It was now only four days until the show opened. The professor had taken every precaution to prevent anyone tampering with the dragon, but if someone should find a way to interfere with it, as they had with the fiery vase, the consequences would be dreadful.

Artie was lost in these thoughts until they neared the Majestic Theatre and Ham gave him a poke.

"Look at that, Artie. Somebody pasted a poster up on that wall. Do you suppose it's for our show?"

"I don't know," Artie replied as they approached for a closer look.

The brightly coloured poster announced a brand new magic show at the Alhambra Theatre on Nicolson Street.

> **COME AND SEE THE WONDERS OF THE ORIENT PERFORMED BY**
>
> # KAIROS
>
> ## THE
>
> # PHARAOH
>
> ### OF THE
>
> # FANTASTIC
>
> ## The Alhambra Theatre
> ### 13th July, 7.00 pm

Underneath was a picture of a man in an Egyptian headdress and oriental robes framed by a background of sand dunes and pyramids. His hands were held out before him in a mystical gesture.

"Look at this, Ham, look!" Artie exclaimed in amazement.

"What is it?" said Ham. "What are you so excited about?"

Artie tapped his finger against the pharaoh's left hand. Kairos was wearing a gold ring decorated with a green jewel inside a triangle.

"That's exactly the same ring the man who dropped the joker was wearing. This Kairos is the villain we've been looking for!"

Ham was puzzled. "Are you saying you spotted this chap at the theatre the night of the explosion?"

"He was wearing that same ring."

"Honestly, Artie, I may not be the most observant sort of fellow, but I think I would have spotted somebody decked out as a pharaoh."

Artie gave an exasperated sigh. "He wasn't dressed like that then. In fact, I'm pretty sure he was wearing dark glasses and a false beard as a disguise."

Ham stared at the picture and was about to ask a question when a voice burst out from behind them. "Oh no! Why did someone have to put that there?"

It was Louise Anderson. She was staring at the poster in such horror you would have thought it was a murder scene. She worked her fingers under one corner of the poster and ripped off a scrap that left most of the picture intact.

"No!" Artie exclaimed. "I recognise that ring. I need to show this to Professor Anderson!"

90

Louise's normally kind features suddenly hardened. "No, you will not. Under no circumstances will you speak to my father of this." She seized a loose edge and tore off another piece. "Well, don't just stand there," she ordered. "Help me to get rid of this!"

Reluctantly Artie obeyed, seizing hold of a flap and ripping the poster apart. Ham followed his lead and soon all that was left was a small heap of shredded paper at their feet. Louise gathered up the pieces and gave the boys a stern look.

"Now remember," she told them, "not a word of this to my father."

Artie and Ham nodded mutely as Louise disappeared into the theatre. Artie felt his head spinning, utterly confused by this rapid turn of events.

"Artie, if that was a clue," Ham frowned, "why did she want to destroy it?"

Artie shook his head. "I don't know, Ham, I really don't. Louise can't be in league with Kairos, can she? Surely she wouldn't help to sabotage her own father's show."

Throughout the morning, as he and Ham carried on with the various jobs Fergus assigned to them, Artie was so upset it made his stomach hurt. He had finally come up with a clue only to be forced to destroy it. He wanted to tell Professor Anderson about the poster, but Louise was so vehemently opposed to this, there was no telling what sort of trouble would be unleashed if he opened his mouth.

At midday they sat down for a break in the back row of theatre seats where Artie had left the tin box containing his lunch. Instead of opening the box he got out his notebook and wrote in it:

Madame Sophonisba – has a grudge against the professor

Kairos – a rival magician. Wants to put the professor out of business? Has the same ring as the Bearded Joker.

He tapped the pencil against the page then snapped the book shut with a sigh of frustration.

Ham could tell his friend was down in the dumps. "No need to be so glum." He took a folded napkin from his pocket and opened it in his lap. "Look, I've got a pair of jam tarts here. You can have one if you like."

"No thanks." Artie didn't even look. "I don't have much of an appetite today." He beat his fist against his knee in frustration. "For the first time we seemed to be making headway and now we're back to the start."

"Artie, this might cheer you up." Ham polished off his tart, then put the other back in his pocket. "I've had the most ingenious idea about our detective agency."

"You mean giving up on it and opening a sweet shop instead?" Artie suggested.

"No, no, of course not. What I mean is that I will write up our adventures and get the stories printed in magazines and newspapers."

"I thought you said writers didn't make any money?"

"Artie, do pay attention. Getting paid for the stories isn't the point. They will generate publicity and attract clients. I've already started on the first one."

He reached into the inside pocket of his jacket and tugged out three sheets of folded paper. He opened them out and did his best to smooth the crumpled pages. "See, here it is – The Adventure of the Stolen Corpses."

Artie grimaced. "That makes it sound pretty gruesome. And didn't you tell me adventure stories were a lot of nonsense that gave me foolish ideas?"

Ham waved the objection aside. "That's because they're made-up stories, about pirates and savages and stuff like that. This is real, and that's what's exciting. Just listen."

He held the pages before him and drew himself up straight, then cleared his throat twice before beginning.

"The Adventure of the Stolen Corpses by Mr Edward Hamilton, a gentleman."

"I don't want to be difficult," said Artie, "but you seem to be making yourself the important one."

"Only because I've gone to all the trouble and hard work of actually writing the thing," Ham retorted. "This writing business is actually very tricky and quite tiring. I had to stop two or three times for refreshment."

"I don't doubt that for a moment."

Ham ignored this. "To resume then. It was a Thursday morning when my good friend Mr Arthur Conan Doyle, a gentleman, approached me with the idea of pursuing an investigation of Edinburgh's graveyards. Good eh?"

Artie grunted non-commitally and his friend continued.

"I remember clearly the buttered toast I had for breakfast and the kippers. These were well cooked by my mother, Mrs Dulcinea Hamilton, a lady of most excellent character, who gives instruction in the piano at the very reasonable rate of three shillings per quarter."

"I'm sure your mother will be very excited to be a part of this literary masterpiece," said Artie patiently.

"It seemed like a good opportunity to advertise her business as well," Ham said practically.

"My mother had just set out to go shopping for our tea. She had it in mind to purchase some cured ham, new potatoes and peas. She knows how to make a delicious mustard sauce and my hopes were high that she intended to prepare such a treat."

"Aren't you being a little slow getting to the plot?" Artie asked.

"Just be patient. Sir Walter Scott's stories take a bit of time to get going too. Now pay attention. I decided to bring some cake along with me in case Mr Doyle required to take sustenance in the course of our investigation."

He stopped and stared expectantly at his friend.

"Well?" Artie prompted. "Carry on."

"I'm afraid that's as far as I got," Ham confessed.

Artie stared at his friend. "But what about those other pages?"

"Oh, they're blank. I brought them along in case inspiration should suddenly strike. So what do you think?"

"I think if we don't crack this case, that story will be our last."

"You should eat something," Ham urged. "If we're going to be investigators as well as stagehands, you need to keep your strength up."

"I suppose you're right." Artie opened the tin lunchbox. What caught his eye, however, was not the cheese sandwich and apple his mother had packed for him, but a folded sheet of paper that had not been there before.

"Hello, what's this?" he wondered, opening the note. It contained a short message in large block letters:

IN SCOBIE'S LANE IS THE ANSWER WHICH ONE SEEKS

"What do you make of this?" He showed the note to Ham.

"Scobie's Lane?" Ham wondered aloud. "I've never heard of it. Why is your mother leaving you strange messages?"

"My mother didn't write this. Somebody slipped it into the box while we were off working."

Ham stared around at the workmen, stagehands and performers scattered about the theatre. "Have you any idea who it might have been?"

Artie shook his head just as a voice hailed him. "Taking a break, Artie?"

It was his father, who had entered the theatre while they were puzzling over the note.

"Father?" said Artie. "I thought you were at work."

"I'm taking a lunch break so I can have a brief consultation with the professor." His father brandished a folder filled with drawings.

Though Charles Doyle was working two jobs, Artie was astonished at the reserves of energy he now appeared to have. His enthusiasm for this new project had put a spring in his step that Artie had not seen in a long while. It gladdened his heart to see him like this and a sudden thought crossed his mind.

"At the Office of Works you have maps of the city, don't you?" he asked.

"More than I can count," his father laughed.

"Have you ever heard of a place called Scobie's Lane?"

Charles Doyle pondered a moment. "I can't say it rings a bell. Are you sure it's in Edinburgh?"

"I can only assume so. Do you think you could find out for me?"

"I'll be sure to check the records when I get back to the office," his father nodded. "In the meantime I must show Professor Anderson my new ideas." With a jaunty wave he strode off and disappeared backstage.

Artie examined the note again and chewed his lip thoughtfully.

"Do you suppose it's some sort of code?" Ham suggested. "You know, if you change all the letters into numbers, shift them around, then change them back, maybe there would be some kind of message."

"No, Ham, I don't think that will work." Artie slipped the note into his pocket. "But I'll tell you what we are going to do." Ham leaned forward expectantly as Artie said, "We're going to get inside the Alhambra Theatre and pay a call on Kairos the Pharaoh of the Fantastic."

11.

A Meeting Among the Pyramids

When they had finished work for the day, Artie and Ham made the short walk to Nicolson Street and the Alhambra Theatre, where the Pharaoh of the Fantastic was soon to open his show. Artie led his friend up an alleyway to the back of the building.

"This sneaking about is all very well," Ham complained, "but how are we going to get inside? Couldn't we just have gone in the front way, claiming we wanted to buy tickets?"

"We can't let Kairos know we're here," said Artie. "I don't want him to suspect that we're on to him."

"No, I suppose we can't have that," Ham agreed. "So what now? This is a bit of a smelly spot to be hanging about in."

"Look, there's a window up there." Artie pointed upwards. "Help me shift this barrel over so I can reach it."

Between them the boys managed to heave the barrel into position and Artie climbed on top. The frame of the window had been painted over so no one had bothered to lock it. The paint was old and flaky, however, so Artie took out his penknife and began chipping away around the edges. Once he had loosened the window a little, he was able to shove it open.

He pulled Ham up beside him and together they climbed through, dropping to the floor on the other side. They found themselves in a small, bare room with a door that led out into a narrow passageway. On tiptoe they started along, alert for any sound. So far the theatre appeared to be deserted.

"What exactly are we looking for?" Ham whispered.

"Anything that will give us a clue to who this Kairos chap really is," Artie replied. "I'm pretty sure he's not really an Egyptian."

"Well, that's a comfort. I wouldn't fancy having him bring a mummy to life and send it chasing after us."

The passage brought them to a flight of wooden stairs. Cautiously mounting the steps, they emerged from the gloom onto the stage, which was lit by the late sunshine filtering through a skylight high overhead.

"I say, this is quite the spectacle." Ham surveyed the impressive set-up before them.

In front of a painted backdrop of sand dunes and a blazing desert sun, three large wooden pyramids had been erected along with a copy of the Sphinx, the famous Egyptian statue of a mythical lion god with the head of a man. Statues of other ancient deities with the heads of various animals stood about like sentries. In the centre of it all a mummy case, painted with colourful hieroglyphics, was laid out flat like a coffin.

"Yes, Kairos is certainly planning to put on a show," agreed Artie. "It might be he doesn't want any competition from Professor Anderson's new illusion."

Ham wandered over to the mummy case. He raised a hand over the lid then hastily snatched it back as a thought occurred to him. "Artie, do you suppose there's a mummy inside here?"

Artie was walking around the Sphinx, which was much smaller than the original in Egypt, but still occupied a large part of the stage.

"No, Ham, it's just a prop," he answered.

"I suppose it's safe to take a look then."

Just as he was opening the lid, both boys stiffened at the sound of a door opening and closing. The voices of two men were approaching from off stage.

"Quick, hide!" warned Artie, diving behind the Sphinx.

He saw Ham clambering into the mummy case and the lid falling shut on top of him. Artie crouched in hiding, listening to the approaching footsteps.

"Yes, this is all very impressive, I'm sure," said one of the men.

He didn't actually sound impressed – but more importantly, the voice was familiar. Artie poked his head in between the Sphinx's outstretched front paws and its chin, just far enough to catch a glimpse of the speaker. He had to stifle a gasp of surprise.

The man talking was Professor Anderson. He was waving his hand about at the pyramids and the painted backdrop.

"This is all so unnecessary," he continued in a pained voice. "There is no need for you to pile up extravagant debts to create this empty fabrication."

A younger man came into view. Even though he was dressed in an ordinary suit, not the garb of a royal Egyptian, Artie recognised him as the man in the poster, Kairos the Pharaoh of the Fantastic.

Artie's thoughts reeled. If these men were such intense rivals – if Kairos was bent on ruining the professor's return to the stage – what were they doing here together?

"The point is," countered the young man, "that all this is mine, not yours."

"Yours perhaps, but based upon what?" demanded the professor. "Upon my talent and hard work, upon everything that I have taught you of the craft and techniques of magic."

"Of course, I appreciate that," Kairos replied, "but I have to find my own way."

"What, by turning your back on your family, on your heritage?"

The young man wheeled sharply away, as though to hide the emotion in his face. "That's your heritage you're speaking of, not mine."

"It is yours too, Johnny," the professor insisted, his tone now almost pleading. "You can take up my mantle and become the new Great Wizard of the North. That is what I have dreamed of for so many years."

"I have a dream of my own and this is it." Kairos leaned against one of the pyramids, as though the argument was draining his strength. "I have no desire to live as an imitation of you."

The professor's face flushed with exasperation. "It's not like that at all. You could carry on in your own way, seek new heights, without abandoning all you have inherited."

As if to emphasise the point, he slammed his hand down violently on the mummy case.

Artie's heart skipped a beat as he expected Ham to

cry out and give himself away. To his relief his friend showed the presence of mind to keep quiet.

The young man faced the professor squarely. "All you see is the path you have laid out before me. Granted, that would be the safe route to follow, but that is not what I want."

"Instead you would rather take this mad gamble?"

"It's my risk to take, not yours," the young man declared stubbornly.

The professor turned and strode rapidly down the length of the stage, his angry footsteps echoing through the theatre.

Artie scrambled backwards to keep out of sight and bumped into a potted palm. The plant swayed and Artie made a desperate grab for it. Clenching his teeth to keep himself from crying out, he managed to right the palm before it could fall.

The professor marched back to confront the younger man once more.

"To what end do you run such a risk?" he demanded. "What if you should fail, as many magicians do? I have suffered a number of disasters and had to rebuild my entire life out of the ruins."

"Then you should be happy with what you've achieved and leave me to follow my own path," snapped Kairos.

Artie poked his head around the Sphinx again and saw the professor's shoulders slump. He suddenly seemed far older than the proud figure Artie had seen commanding the centre of a stage.

"When I retire for good, as soon I must, what will become of the legend of the Great Wizard then? In a few short years some new magician will capture the imagination and affection of the public, in all likelihood one not half as able. I will be forgotten, like an old discarded handbill."

Kairos took a half-step towards the older man, his attitude softening. He stretched out a hand in a gesture that was almost beseeching. "I am sure that will never be."

The air between the two was charged with something much more than rivalry. Strained as it was, it was a deep and painful affection. For the first time Artie noticed a resemblance between the two in the nose and the mouth. The truth struck him like a lightning flash. Kairos was not simply a competitor – he was the Great Wizard's son!

He understood now why Louise wouldn't let him tell the professor about the poster and the ring. She was afraid it would exacerbate the bad feeling between her father and her brother.

The Great Wizard drew himself up stiffly. "I shall not be replaced by you at any rate. My new illusion will be the talk of the whole country and no one will give a second thought to Kairos the Pharaoh and his antics." With that he turned and marched off the stage.

Artie watched as his son stared after him. The young man's jaw tightened as he bit back an angry reply. He took a few moments to calm himself before he too departed.

Artie waited until he was sure both men were gone before he slipped out of hiding. Tapping gently on the mummy case, he called softly, "It's alright, Ham. You can come out now."

When there was no reply Artie raised his voice. "Ham, you haven't fallen asleep in there, have you?"

It occurred to him that it would be just like Ham to doze off in the middle of the heated confrontation between the two magicians. Taking a firm grip on the lid, he lifted it up.

His jaw dropped and he let out a gasp.

The mummy case was completely empty.

Ham had disappeared.

12.

Utterly Impossible

"Ham?" Artie's voice sounded lost and lonely in the middle of the deserted stage. Suddenly anxious, he circled the mummy case, peering at it from all sides, but he saw no way Ham could have slipped out without being spotted. He peered behind the palm trees and pyramids, hoping desperately for some sign of his friend, but he was completely alone.

Artie's mind began to race through all manner of possibilities. Perhaps Kairos really was the villain he had first imagined him to be? Perhaps he had spirited Ham away and now held him prisoner, with who knew what fate in store? Worst of all, might Ham really have disappeared into thin air, never to be seen again?

He walked to the edge of the stage and gazed out over the rows of empty seats, wondering what he should do. Then he suddenly heard a cough.

He spun about, but there was no one in sight. Then, from below his feet came a thump. Looking down into the orchestra pit, he saw a door open at the base of the stage. A moment later Ham tottered out, blinking about him in confusion.

"Ham!" Artie exclaimed.

Ham started and looked up. "Artie! It's you!" He shook his head in bewilderment. "I had no idea what had become of me."

Artie ran down the steps at the side of the stage to join his friend.

"Thank goodness you're safe, Ham! I was starting to imagine the most awful things. What happened?"

"It was the queerest thing ever. I lay down in the mummy case, doing my best to keep quiet. I couldn't make out what those chaps were saying, but when one of them thumped the lid, some sort of trapdoor opened right under me. I went sliding down a chute and landed on a mattress in the dark."

Artie laughed out of sheer relief. "It must be some trick device created for a disappearing act."

"Well, it was pitch black and I had no idea where I was," Ham continued. "I felt my way around the wall until I came to a door. I stepped through and found myself here."

Artie gave his friend a clap on the shoulder. "I think

we'd best get out of here before anything else happens."

They retraced their route back to the open window and climbed out into the alley. Along the way Artie explained what he had overheard.

"It does sound like there's a lot of bad feeling between them," said Ham. "Kairos might be trying to wreck the professor's show and Louise might be helping him to do it."

"Yes, that's possible," Artie conceded.

As they came around the front of the theatre a grey-haired old lady in a plaid bonnet and faded blue dress blocked their way. She was carrying a basket of dried flowers.

She hailed them in a cracked voice. "Ah, here's a pair of young gentlemen. Would you care to buy some flowers?"

"We're actually in a bit of a hurry." Artie tried to weave a path around her.

"I have lavender here, rosemary and marjoram," the flower seller insisted.

"No, thanks," said Ham. "We don't have any use for flowers."

"No use for flowers?" the old lady called after them as they walked away. "Surely you know a pretty young lady who would welcome them as a gift."

The boys hurried out of earshot.

"She was a bit pushy, wasn't she?" Ham increased his pace to make sure the old lady couldn't follow them.

"She looked very poor," Artie surmised. "I suppose she's doing her best to make a living."

Neither of them looked back to see the old lady's sharp green eyes following them as they walked off down the street.

By the time Artie got home the rest of the family had already sat down to a dinner of mutton stew. His mother hurried him to his seat and ladled a helping onto his plate.

"Artie," Lottie was trying her best to sound like her mother, "it's very bad of you to stay out so late. You promised Connie you'd draw her a picture of the white rabbit from *Alice in Wonderland*."

"You promised," Connie agreed, nodding sternly.

"Yes, I will." Artie took up his cutlery. "Just let me have something to eat first."

"I had no idea the professor expected you to work such long hours," said his mother disapprovingly. "I hope you're keeping up with your school work."

"Of course I am." Artie turned to Mr Doyle, who was soaking up his gravy with a slice of bread. "Father, did you find out about Scobie's Lane?" Artie had looked through several maps of Edinburgh and found no trace of the mysterious street.

Charles Doyle paused with the bread halfway to his mouth. He tapped a fist against his head. "I forgot all about it," he apologised. "My head is so full of art right now. I do assure you Artie that I will look into the matter thoroughly tomorrow."

"Oh, and Artie," his mother reached into a pocket of her apron and pulled out an envelope, "someone slipped this under the door for you."

Artie saw his name written on the envelope and inside was a note from the professor.

Mr Doyle,

I shall arrive at six AM promptly to collect you and Mr Hamilton. I wish you to join me on a mission of the utmost importance.

J.H. Anderson.

Six in the morning! thought Artie. Ham would not be pleased about that.

Sure enough, Ham was still yawning when they set out for the warehouse in a one-horse carriage driven by

Professor Anderson himself. There was a chill in the air, and a haar from the river was creeping up the road, casting a murky halo around the gas street lamps. Ham tucked his hands under his arms and bowed his head so low his face disappeared under the brim of his cap.

"Honestly, Ham, you're such a mole." Artie grinned. "You'd think you'd never been out in daylight before."

Ham stifled another yawn. "If you don't mind my asking, sir, where are we going?"

"To the workshop," Anderson replied. "This is an important day. The dragon has been completed with all the mechanisms and effects operating to perfection."

"And safely?" queried Artie.

"Yes, safely, of course," the professor answered rather curtly. "This morning we are transporting it to the Majestic."

"It's a pity Mr Galbraith couldn't just climb into the blessed thing and walk it down to the theatre himself," said Ham, rubbing his eyes.

"I hardly think that the populace of Edinburgh would take kindly to a full-grown dragon marching down the street breathing fire," replied the professor. "Besides, it is too large to fit through the warehouse doors. Last night I supervised its dismantling and saw the separated components nailed securely shut in a dozen stout wooden crates."

"We don't have to move them ourselves, do we?" asked Artie, concerned at the prospect of so much heavy lifting.

"No, no," the professor assured him. "We are merely here to open the place up and make sure all is ready. When Mr Galbraith and his assistants arrive they will transport the boxes by wagon to the theatre. There the magnificent creature will be reassembled in all its glory."

"Then what do you need us for?" Ham asked blearily.

"The men and I will be fully occupied with the loading and unloading. I would like you two here to keep a close watch for any sign of trouble."

"We'll do just that, sir," Artie promised.

The clopping of the horse's hooves echoed off the empty streets until they arrived outside the warehouse. The professor tethered the animal to a post and led the way to the securely fastened doors. He took out his keys and one by one released the three iron locks. Artie noticed that each key had to be inserted in a special manner.

When all the locks were released, the Professor Anderson pocketed his keys and thrust the doors open. He strode inside with the boys at his heels but almost at once came to a stunned halt.

"No!" he cried. "No! This is utterly impossible!"

The only light came from the open doorway and the small window at the back, but even in the dimness it was plain to see that there was no dragon and no pile of crates waiting to be carted away. There was nothing except a few work tables scattered with tools.

Ham gasped and blinked as if trying to shake off a bad dream. "What's happened to the dragon?"

The professor pointed an unsteady finger. "The crates were right there in the middle of the floor."

"They're not there now," said Artie. "Are you sure your men haven't already taken them away?"

"I locked the doors myself last night." Almost in a trance, Anderson walked to the centre of the floor and stood there in amazement. "No one could have entered without these keys of mine. This is the only set."

Casting a searching eye around the big room, Artie noticed something. "Look there, by the window!" he exclaimed, running forward.

A ladder was propped against the far wall right under the window. It hadn't been obvious in the dim light, but as soon as he reached it he realised something else. "The bars have gone. Somebody must have filed through them."

The professor hurried over to join him and frowned at the open space, muttering, "That would have taken all night."

Artie scrambled up the ladder and stuck his head through the open window. The narrow street beyond lay in the shadow of the surrounding buildings but some distance off to his right, he spotted something – a wagon, painted bright red with brilliant yellow wheels. It was loaded up with large wooden crates.

"It's there!" he exclaimed. "There in the street!"

"What's that you say, lad?" asked the professor.

"The dragon!" Artie answered excitedly. "The crates have all been loaded onto a wagon out here."

Even as he spoke, the wagon began to move away. He could just make out a single hunched figure in the driver's seat.

"Come back here!" Artie yelled. "Stop! Thief!"

13.

Even More Impossible

Artie launched himself through the window and dropped to the street on the other side. As he started off after the wagon he heard Ham calling out, "Artie, wait for me!"

There was no time to waste. He plunged into the shadowy maze of warehouses and factories, pursuing the wagon through a brick archway. He found himself in a cobbled courtyard with two further exits and no sign of the wagon. Halting, he strained his ears to listen.

Sure enough, from off to his right came the clip-clop of hooves and the rumble of wheels. Pelting across the courtyard, he dived into an alleyway, where he glimpsed the wagon trundling away.

The driver must have seen him for he gave a crack of his whip and the horse broke into a trot. As Artie tried to give chase, he tripped on a loose cobblestone and went sprawling flat on the ground. Bruised and winded, he heaved himself up on one elbow just as Ham arrived, red-faced and wheezing.

"I say, I wish you'd stop bolting off like that," he puffed as he helped Artie to his feet.

"What else was I to do?" Artie rubbed his bruised shoulder. "We have to get the dragon back."

He broke off as, with a clatter of hoofbeats, Professor Anderson's carriage swung into view. He slowed down enough for the boys to leap aboard then demanded, "Which way did the villains go?"

"Up there, sir – that lane to the right," pointed Artie.

With a flick of the reins, the professor sped his horse in pursuit. They followed a long cobbled road then swerved round a corner, where they were brought up short.

The red wagon with the yellow wheels lay sideways across a narrow lane, blocking the route. The professor pulled up just in time to avoid a collision and gave a snort of exasperation.

"This is the wagon, sir." Artie gaped in surprise. "Except that the driver, the horse and the dragon have all disappeared."

"The rogue must have untethered the horse and ridden off," said Ham, "though I'm blessed if I can see how he took those crates with him."

"No time to lose!" The professor shook the reins.

"You two give chase on foot while I try to find another way around."

The boys hopped down and raced off down the tangle of streets, but the thief was long gone. When the professor caught up with them Ham was doubled over, sucking in breath.

Anderson grimaced. "He's made good his escape. But how did he carry the crates? There are at least a dozen of them and it would take two strong men to lift even one."

"I don't see how he could have done it," Artie agreed.

Ham pulled out a kerchief to wipe the sweat from his brow. "I suppose, then, that this is even more impossible."

Back at the warehouse the professor slumped down on a stool, burying his face in his hands.

Artie gazed helplessly about him, hoping to glimpse some clue as to how the astonishing robbery was carried out. While the thief had certainly sawed through the bars to get in through the window, there was no way the boxes containing the components of the dragon would have fitted through the narrow space. And yet he had seen them loaded on the wagon on the street outside, only to find that they had vanished once he and Ham caught up with the fleeing vehicle.

When Laurence Galbraith and the two engineers

showed up with their own wagon to transport the dragon to the theatre, Professor Anderson was still bent over in abject despair.

"Professor, what's happened?" gasped Galbraith, staring about at the empty warehouse.

"A robbery!" groaned the professor. "An impossible robbery!"

Artie told the men what had happened and Galbraith shook his head dolefully. "The professor was the last to leave. I was with him when he locked up last night and I know those doors couldn't have been opened."

"I can't see any explanation," said Artie.

"Obviously the professor can't either." Ham glanced pityingly at Anderson.

"There's nothing for it then," Galbraith concluded unhappily. "We shall have to call in the police."

When the Edinburgh Constabulary arrived an hour later it was in the form of someone the two boys knew well.

"Constable McCorkle!" Artie exclaimed at the sight of the familiar figure in his long police coat and top hat.

"That's Sergeant McCorkle now, Mr Doyle." The policeman proudly pointed to the stripes on his sleeve. "I received a promotion on account of the very important part I played in that matter of the gravediggers."

"Very well deserved, I'm sure," Artie complimented him.

"This sounds like a rum business and that's a fact." McCorkle raised an eyebrow as he surveyed the scene of the crime. "I take it that sad-looking gentleman on the stool is the aggrieved party."

"Yes, that's Professor Anderson," said Artie.

"The Great Wizard of the North," added Ham. "We've been working for him."

"Have you indeed?" queried the policeman. "Let me find out what the noted entertainer has to say for himself."

McCorkle took a statement from the dazed professor. Artie couldn't help worrying that this blow might prove too much for the aging magician to recover from. He and Ham chipped in to confirm his story as McCorkle noted it down with many dubious noises and much sceptical eyebrow raising.

When the statement was complete the policeman closed his notebook. "A word with you please, Mr Doyle." He led Artie to a corner where the magician could not overhear.

"Now, Mr Doyle, you have been known to indulge in some flights of the imagination, but overall I judge you to be a young gentleman of sound character."

"Thank you, constable – I mean sergeant. I hope I am."

"However, this business of dragons, impassable doors

and disappearing crates is simply not credible. I have to assume the tale has become garbled in the telling."

"Oh, no," said Artie. "He's telling it just as it happened."

"Mr Doyle, it is plain impossible," said McCorkle gravely, "which means he must have fabricated the entire incident."

"But why would he do that?" Artie objected.

"As a means to publicise his forthcoming magic show, I suppose. Publicity is the very lifeblood of these theatre folk. They seek it in any way, regardless of the consequences."

"Sergeant, I assure you…" Artie began, but McCorkle raised a hand to silence him.

"Mr Doyle, I advise you and your friend not to implicate yourselves any further in this fanciful matter. Drawing the Edinburgh Constabulary into such nonsense might well be considered an offence, so I shall report it to my superiors as a misunderstanding."

Turning on his heel, the policeman marched out just as Louise arrived and rushed to her father's side. When she heard about the robbery, she gazed about her in disbelief.

"Mr Galbraith and I have checked every corner," Professor Anderson told her. "There are no secret passages in the walls, no trapdoors in the floor, and the roof is completely solid with no way through. I can't see how the theft was accomplished."

"Whatever is to be done?" Louise wondered, laying a hand on his arm.

"There's nothing that can be done," Professor Anderson sighed, as she led him out. "There will be no *Princess and the Dragon*, no triumphant return to the stage."

Artie paused before following everyone else outside, and looked back at the deserted warehouse. Something about it seemed different from when they had first arrived.

"What's the matter?" asked Ham.

"I don't know." Artie shook his head. "Something about this place isn't right. I just can't put my finger on what it is."

Once everyone was outside, the professor locked up.

"There's hardly much point in these wonderful locks now," he reflected gloomily, slipping the keys back into his pocket.

As the party moved away, Ham drew Artie aside. "McCorkle's not going to be much use, is he?"

"No," said Artie. "He doesn't believe a word of it, and I can't say that I blame him. This is going to be the ruin of the professor."

"Don't worry, Artie," Ham told him with an excited gleam in his eye. "I have an absolutely brilliant plan."

"A plan? What are you talking about?"

"Leave it to me, Artie. I know exactly how we're going to solve this crime."

14.

Berrybus on the Trail

While everyone else returned to the theatre, Artie and Ham made a round trip by horse-drawn tram to fetch Ham's enormous black mastiff Berrybus. They led the hound to the warehouse, where Ham offered the reward of an aniseed cake – his favourite treat – to coax him into sniffing around the outside walls and pavements.

"I'm really not sure about this." Artie tried not to sound too sceptical.

"Artie, believe me, it's genius, pure genius," Ham declared with glowing confidence. "You know how bloodhounds are used to track people down."

"Yes, I've heard about that," Artie agreed, "but Berrybus isn't a bloodhound."

"He's still a dog, and all dogs have a keen sense of smell. Don't you, boy?" He scratched his pet fondly behind the ear.

Berrybus gazed hopefully up at him, his mouth hanging open and his tongue lolling.

"Not yet," said Ham firmly, though he couldn't help smiling. "No more cake until you sniff out the culprits."

Reluctantly the huge hound returned to snuffling around the building.

"He doesn't seem to be making much progress," Artie observed.

"Give him time. The robbery only took place this morning, so the trail is still fresh. I'm sure he'll pick it up."

As he was speaking, Berrybus abruptly perked up. Tugging on his lead, he led them around the back of the warehouse to the street where Artie had spotted the escaping wagon. He sniffed the ground under the window then raised his nose into the air.

"You see," said Ham gleefully, "he's on to something already."

With a sudden bound Berrybus lurched forward, almost yanking Ham off his feet. He gripped the lead tightly with both hands as the dog dragged him along the street.

"You may be right, Ham." Artie hurried after them. "He's certainly excited about something."

When they came to a corner the dog stopped briefly to sniff the air before charging off again.

"Go to it, boy!" Ham encouraged him. "You find those robbers!"

Berrybus led them briskly out of the warehouse area and into a street of shops and houses. Artie's heart was pounding at the prospect of them bursting in on a den of thieves. The sight of the huge dog would probably be enough to make the criminals surrender.

Berrybus ploughed to a stop in front of a shop window. He laid his great paws against the glass and slobbered over it with his tongue.

It was a bakery and in the window, among the buns and tarts, was a tray of aniseed cakes.

Artie felt the exhilaration drain out of him. "Well, Ham, if we ever do open a detective agency, I suppose our offices could be above a baker's shop."

"Oh Berrybus," groaned Ham, "can't you think of anything but your stomach?"

The dog gazed up at him so appealingly that he gave in and fed him another bit of cake out of his pocket.

"Don't feel down," Artie consoled his friend. "It was worth a try."

"Yes, I suppose so," Ham sighed.

"We'd better take him home and get back to the theatre," Artie suggested.

When they arrived back at the Majestic Theatre they were surprised to find the old flower seller standing outside the door, her back bent over her basket of flowers. She blocked the way when they tried to enter, thrusting a handful of heather at them.

"Won't you buy some flowers, dearie?" she wheedled.

"Not now," said Artie testily. "We need to get inside."

He tried to get around her but she blocked his path, moving very nimbly for someone who looked so infirm.

"Here, are you chasing us all over town?" Ham demanded.

Artie blinked, his suspicions aroused. "You're right, Ham. This is the second time she's popped up right in front of us."

"Just selling flowers," the old woman whined. "You wouldn't deny me the chance to make a few pennies, would you?"

"I'm not so sure that's what you're doing," said Artie. "In fact, I don't think you're even who you say you are."

The old lady gave a surprisingly youthful chuckle. Straightening up, she pulled off her bonnet and grey wig, freeing the bright red hair that tumbled down about her shoulders.

"It's me, you sillies – Rowena!"

Artie was so surprised all he could do was repeat, "Rowena?"

Ham let out a groan. "You! Why are you sneaking around after us?"

"I knew you were up to something," said the girl in an annoyingly superior tone, "snooping about, holding secret conversations in dark corners, so I decided to follow you. You're trying to find out who's been causing the accidents to the professor's show, aren't you?"

"Well, yes," Artie conceded.

Ham stared at her accusingly. "Was it you?"

"Oh don't be such a goose," scoffed Rowena. "Of course it wasn't me."

"That was a good disguise," Artie admitted. "But we still need to get inside."

"There's no point," Rowena informed him. "The professor was so upset that his dragon has been stolen, he sent everyone home early and closed the place up."

Giving Rowena an unfriendly look, Ham tried the door. "Yes, it's locked."

"I'm so sorry for the professor," said Artie. "He's quite crushed by this business." He felt doubly unhappy because the magician had been relying on them to prevent something like this from happening and they had let him down.

"Yes, things are getting very serious," said Rowena decisively. "It's time the three of us put our heads together."

"I'm not putting my head anywhere near yours." Ham wrinkled his nose in distaste.

In spite of himself, Artie was inclined to agree with Rowena. "She's only suggesting we compare notes and try to solve this mystery together." It occurred to him that if the girl could disguise herself so brilliantly, she might have some useful talents after all. "It might not be a bad idea at that."

"Good!" Beaming, Rowena turned and yelled loudly, "Clatter!"

In answer to the summons, a thin, worried-looking woman in a lace bonnet appeared round the corner of the theatre.

"Clatter, please fetch Mr Lampkin," Rowena instructed.

The anxious woman disappeared. Rowena laid down her basket of flowers and pulled a wet sponge out of her bag, which she used to wipe off the make-up that had made her face appear old and wrinkled.

A few moments later, Clatter emerged from a side street in an open horse-drawn carriage driven by a moustachioed man in a bowler hat and overcoat. The vehicle pulled up beside them and they climbed aboard.

"This is Clatter," Rowena indicated the woman, "and this is her friend Mr Lampkin, the carriage driver."

Mr Lampkin doffed his hat in greeting.

"That is *Miss* Clatter," the woman corrected. "Really Rowena, you must introduce persons properly."

Rowena carried on without acknowledging that she

had spoken. "Clatter, these are my dear friends Arturo and Eduardo."

"That's Arthur Conan Doyle, ma'm." Artie offered his hand.

"Edward Hamilton," said Ham. "And to be honest," he added with a sidelong glance at Rowena, "I had no idea we were friends."

"Of course we're friends," insisted the girl as they settled into their seats. "We're all members of the same theatrical fraternity."

"Even if we're not all *phenomena*," Artie joked.

Rowena did not look amused. She said tartly, "Mr Lampkin, would you take us home, please?"

As they set off, Artie wondered why the girl should have a private carriage ready at her beck and call. He remembered hearing that her parents were quite rich, but realised he knew very little about her.

"Does this vehicle belong to you?" he asked.

"Goodness, no," said Rowena. "It belongs to Mr Lampkin, but I hire him quite often to get about town." Leaning in towards the boys, she whispered mischievously, "Frankly, I think he makes himself available just so he can see Clatter."

"Rowena!" Miss Clatter exclaimed in shock. "Such talk!"

Rowena settled back in her seat, giggling.

Ham slouched forward and frowned at her. "You know, I'm not sure we need your help. Artie and I are quite experienced at this sort of thing."

"Are you?" Rowena retorted. "You were completely fooled by my disguise, so what chance do you have of unmasking a villain?"

Ham folded his arms and grumped stubbornly.

"It might be helpful to have another point of view," said Artie.

"I'm glad to hear you say that, Arturo." Rowena leaned forward again and lowered her voice. "Because, frankly, I think we all know who's behind this."

15.

The Phenomenon
Holds Forth

For the rest of the journey Rowena would say nothing further about her suspicions. She made it clear that she didn't want to discuss the matter in front of Miss Clatter. A ten-minute ride brought them to Moray Place, where the grand houses were a far cry from the tenement flats the boys were used to. When they had disembarked, Mr Lampkin doffed his hat to them again and drove off.

Rowena led the way up the front steps of her large, three-storey town house. They walked into a spacious hallway, richly carpeted and decorated with paintings and plaster statues in the Greek and Roman style.

"This way to the parlour," said Rowena. "Clatter, could you fetch us some tea?"

"Yes, Rowena," Miss Clatter replied. "And please

make sure these boys don't touch anything." With a sniff she took herself off.

"What was that about not touching anything?" said Artie.

"Oh, she is such an old fusspot," Rowena laughed. "She's terrified in case anything gets broken while my parents are away."

The parlour was almost bigger than the whole of the Doyles' flat. Artie looked about and saw a number of delicate porcelain figurines perched on shelves and works of Chinese and Indian art hanging on the walls.

Rowena threw herself down in a large comfy chair and gestured to the boys to do likewise.

"Your parents aren't about then?" Ham settled himself down on the sofa and sank into the soft cushions.

"No, they're travelling," said Rowena. "They travel quite a lot, you know, because they are the most fascinating people. They're probably visiting one of my father's gold mines in Peru or attending some glamorous party in Venice."

"When did you last see them?" Artie walked around the room, taking a closer look at the expensive ornaments.

Rowena's smile wavered. "I can't recall exactly. I've been away at school in Switzerland and by the time I got home they had already left on one of their trips."

"So you're here all on your own then?" asked Artie.

"Well, some of the servants do live in," said Rowena airily. "And there's Clatter, of course. She's supposed to be my governess, but honestly, she hasn't a clue."

Artie wondered what it must be like to stay in a house as big as this with no family around you.

"How did you get involved with Professor Anderson?" he asked.

Rowena tossed her hair. "Well, I've always been fascinated by the theatre. At the Montecelli College for Young Gentlewomen I've been studying drama and music." Her face brightened. "Would you like me to play something for you?" She made a move towards a violin that was propped up on a chair in the corner.

"Oh please don't!" groaned Ham.

Rowena sat back down and scowled at him.

"Perhaps later," said Artie. "You were telling us about Professor Anderson?"

"Oh, yes, yes," the girl resumed. "I heard he was coming out of retirement and that he was trying to raise money to reopen the Majestic Theatre. You learn about such things when you move in the right circles. Well, I arranged with my father's lawyer to release some funds to the professor and he was so grateful he gave me a part in the show."

Artie had no doubt that accepting Rowena into the company was the price the professor had to pay for the donation.

Ham, meanwhile, was getting so comfy on the luxurious sofa that his mood was beginning to mellow. "Everything seems to have worked out for you then," he commented affably.

"It is only a small part," said Rowena, "but you have to begin somewhere, and I do get to sing. And I shall be billed as the Theatrical Phenomenon, of course."

"Of course." Artie humoured her.

Rowena squinted at him. "So what about you two? Right from the start I was pretty sure there was something fishy going on."

"On the recommendation of a mutual acquaintance," Artie explained, "the professor brought us in to investigate these suspicious accidents."

"Yes, everybody's aware of them." Rowena nodded sagely. "Some people have even fled the show in fear of their lives."

Before Artie could respond, Miss Clatter entered carrying a large silver tea tray. She laid it down on the table and was about to pick up the teapot when Rowena waved her away.

"That's quite alright, Clatter," she said dismissively. "We can pour for ourselves."

Miss Clatter backed out the door, glancing about the room to assure herself that the visitors had done no damage.

Artie sat down beside Ham while Rowena poured the tea. "Add milk and sugar to taste," she said.

Ham helped himself to a meringue from the cake stand Clatter had provided. Rowena took a ladylike sip from her china cup then set it down gently on its saucer.

"Now, tell me about this vanishing dragon," she said. "I hear it disappeared under the most curious circumstances."

Ham rolled his eyes. "That's putting it mildly."

"On the face of it the whole thing appears completely impossible," explained Artie. "For a start, the locks on the warehouse door were specially designed by the professor to be tamper-proof and he has the only set of keys."

"We know the robbers came in through the window," said Ham. "The bars had been cut away and they even left the ladder they climbed down."

"And clearly, if they had somehow got hold of another set of keys," Artie continued, "they wouldn't have bothered messing around with the window. They could simply have come in through the door."

"So the culprits entered by the window and exited with the dragon," said Rowena. "I'm not sure that I see what's so puzzling about that."

"The puzzle," Artie swallowed a mouthful of tea, "is that the window is about eight feet above the floor

135

and so small a grown man would have trouble squeezing through it."

"The dragon was packed into a lot of big wooden boxes," continued Ham, "and they couldn't possibly fit through that tiny space." He paused and helped himself to another cake. "It really vexes the brain, doesn't it?"

"And yet," said Rowena, "the thing was done – somehow."

"That's not even the end of it," said Artie. "I saw the crates loaded onto the back of a wagon in the street outside the window."

"We chased after it," said Ham through a mouthful of sponge.

"On foot at first," said Artie, "and then in the professor's carriage. But when we caught up with the wagon, the horse and the driver were gone."

"And so were the boxes," added Ham. "It's really—"

"Impossible," finished Artie. "Simply impossible."

Rowena's expression was grave. "Do you know what it suggests to me?"

"No, what?" said Ham.

"Yes, what?" said Artie.

Rowena rose dramatically to her feet and struck a pose, as though facing an audience. "It suggests a supernatural agency."

"You mean like magic?" said Artie. "Real magic?"

"Or witchcraft?" Ham inquired in a shaky voice.

"Exactly!" Rowena affirmed, waving her finger in the air. "Mark my words, we are up against dark forces. And that suggests one obvious candidate – Madame Sophonisba."

Artie and Ham exchanged glances.

"She's certainly a scary old bird," Ham agreed.

"I know she claimed she could walk through walls," said Artie, "but the professor says she's a fake."

"Is that so?" Rowena raised a sceptical eyebrow. "Perhaps he's mistaken. If she has laid a hex on him, that would explain his run of bad luck."

"There's something in that, you know." The tea and cakes were making Ham more and more agreeable.

"And if she can dematerialise and pass through a solid wall," Rowena continued, "she could probably transport the dragon in the same way."

"I suppose it does make a sort of sense," Artie admitted. "But we can hardly go to the police with a story like that. Sergeant McCorkle already thinks we've made up the whole thing."

"Then we'll pursue our own investigation." Rowena pointed to each of the boys in turn, as though she were recruiting them to her team.

"You mean investigate Madame Sophonisba?" Ham shrank away from her pointing finger.

Rowena nodded. "Exactly. I've learned a few things about her – I move in those sort of circles, you know. She has a big house in Cramond and inside there's supposed to be some sort of temple."

"A temple?" said Ham. "That sounds a bit creepy."

"I imagine there'll be a nasty punishment in store if she catches us trying to break into any sort of holy place," said Artie.

"There's no need to break in," Rowena explained. "She likes to invite rich people into her home so she can persuade them to contribute to her cause. What we need is a cunning disguise. Follow me!"

She led the boys out of the parlour and up a richly carpeted stairway to an upper floor. She threw open a door and beckoned them inside.

The room beyond was filled with racks and racks of clothing – but not just any clothes. These were theatrical costumes: silk dresses, oriental robes, fur coats, striped blazers; and every imaginable sort of hat: turbans, fezzes, sombreros, feather headdresses.

The boys wandered about, amazed at the variety of costumes.

"Now, what would best suit our plan?" Rowena wondered, examining rack after rack.

"How's this?" Ham picked up a hat with earflaps and clapped it onto his head.

"That's called a deerstalker," said Rowena, "and it doesn't suit you at all."

"It makes you look like a gamekeeper," laughed Artie. "Take it off."

Ham tossed the deerstalker aside and tried on a top hat instead.

Artie donned a bishop's mitre and regarded himself in the full-length mirror. "I think I look rather spiffy in this," he announced.

A gleeful cry from Rowena made him turn around.

"I've got just the thing!" She waved a pair of fur hats triumphantly in the air. "Does either of you speak Russian?"

16.

The Countess Oligovsky

The following morning they travelled in Mr Lampkin's carriage to Madame Sophonisba's house in Cramond, half an hour outside of town. A mysterious atmosphere hung over their journey, enhanced by a stately ruin they passed on the way and the tangy sea air wafting in from the Forth.

Miss Clatter had been ordered to remain behind. "We simply can't have her clucking about the place like an overexcited hen," Rowena explained.

"Please wait for us here, Mr Lampkin," she said when they arrived. "We shouldn't be more than an hour."

He nodded silently. As they walked up the driveway Artie realised he had never heard the man speak a word.

"Does he ever say anything?" he asked.

"Not much," Rowena replied. "It's a pleasant relief from Clatter and her endless chatter."

The girl was decked out in a luxuriant black wig, a mink coat with a trailing ermine wrap and Cossack-style boots. She was wearing make-up, which, along with her upright posture and overbearing manner, made her appear much older than her fourteen years.

Under their fur hats the boys had been supplied with long, bushy wigs that covered their ears and much of their faces. They wore red woollen coats fastened with gold buttons and belted with leather.

"Do we really have to be trussed up like this?" Ham complained. "I swear I'm going to melt in the heat."

"Really, Eduardo, you must bear up," Rowena reprimanded him. "The soul of a good performance is conviction."

Gable windows and twin turrets gave the house the appearance of an ancient palace where the king of a bygone age might have lived. Above the front door in large Gothic letters they saw the name:

Templemoor

It looked to Artie like the kind of place where all sorts of nefarious deeds might take place, like those in the spooky stories of Mr Edgar Allan Poe that gave him such enjoyable shivers.

Rowena gestured to Artie to tug on the bell pull. In answer to the jangling, a broad-shouldered maid with thick black eyebrows ushered them into the hallway.

"You are the Countess Oligovsky?" she inquired.

Rowena threw back her head. "You are most correct," she acknowledged in a thick Russian accent. "You will be admitting us to your mistress."

The previous day Rowena had sent a message to Madame Sophonisba, claiming to be a visiting Russian noblewoman who had heard of the lady mystic's unique gifts. She said she was keen to witness an example of her powers and promptly received an invitation to call upon her this morning.

Beckoning them inside, the maid led them past some garish paintings of cats and parakeets cavorting in a jungle. At the end of a long hall she ushered them into the parlour, where Madame Sophonisba was seated along with a pair of guests. Artie recognised the red-faced man and the bird-like woman who had attended Madame Sophonisba when she made her dramatic entrance at the theatre. All three stood to greet the new arrivals.

"Countess Oligovsky, what a privilege it is to welcome you to my home and my sanctuary." Madame Sophonisba's voice was so oily and ingratiating, Artie could hardly believe this was the same woman who had screeched such awful warnings at Professor Anderson.

"Even in my far-off estate of Ngovny-Pdolsk," Rowena declared grandly, "we hear of Madame Sophonisba."

Madame Sophonisba indicated her companions. "Please allow me to introduce my friends and disciples, Sir Merriot Ruthven and Lady Winderbrook."

"An honour, I'm sure, ma'm," said Sir Merriot gruffly.

Rowena haughtily raised her nose in the air and presented him with her outstretched hand. Looking discomfited by the gesture, Ruthven bent and quickly kissed it. He straightened up immediately and tugged at his waistcoat with a throaty, "Hrumph!"

Lady Winderbrook's hands fluttered excitedly. "Oh, Countess, how delightful to make your acquaintance," she twittered.

"These are manservants, Igor and Ivan." Rowena gestured towards the two boys as though they were of little importance.

Madame Sophonisba quirked a curious eyebrow. "Manservants? They appear to be little more than boys."

"No, they are from eastern Yakutsk," Rowena responded with curt authority. "Everyone there is very small. Also very stupid. They speak no English at all. They barely comprehend Russian tongue."

This part of their cover story was Artie's idea. It had occurred to him that if Madame Sophonisba and her friends thought they spoke no English, they would be more likely to let slip some unguarded remark that might provide a clue.

"Indeed?" Madame Sophonisba responded politely. "That must be most trying for you."

"Weak minds but strong backs," said Rowena. "It is ever so."

Sir Merriot Ruthven was pouring himself a large glass of brandy from a decanter. "Impossible to get good help these days," he agreed.

"Shall we be seated?" Madame Sophonisba suggested.

As she and her guests sat down, Artie and Ham looked for a pair of comfy chairs for themselves.

"*Niet! Pstovno babursk!*" Rowena spat at them crossly.

She waved them towards a space on the floor by the fireplace where they settled themselves cross-legged.

"*Ignoski niet dubukov!*" she scolded them.

None of them actually knew a word of Russian, but Artie was impressed at the convincing gibberish Rowena was able to spout. He and Ham hung their heads to show they had taken the rebuke to heart.

"If they are allowed on furniture," Rowena clarified to their hostess, "they will take over whole house. Hahaha!"

The other guests joined in with her laughter.

When everyone was settled, Lady Winderbrook asked in her small, piping voice, "So, countess, what brings you to Edinburgh?"

"Upon death of my husband Count Oligovsky,"

144

Rowena explained airily, "he leaves me enormous fortune – simply enormous. What am I to do with vast wealth? I know! I travel world seeking out lost secrets of ancient lands. I make acquaintance of only most fascinating people."

"Oh, Madame Sophonisba is an extremely fascinating person," said Lady Winderbrook, "and she has uncovered many wonderful secrets."

"Remarkable woman," Sir Merriot affirmed, raising his brandy glass in salute to his hostess, "remarkable."

Madame Sophonisba modestly waved their compliments aside. "It is not I who should be praised but my patroness, the great goddess Astarte."

"Yes, tell me more of this most mysterious Aztarky," said Rowena.

Artie couldn't help admiring Rowena's performance. Not only was she playing her part to perfection, she was also enjoying herself hugely.

"*Astarte*," Madame Sophonisba corrected, "is the great goddess of the ancient land of Phoenicia, where she was worshipped for thousands of years. All the secrets of the world, and all of time, both past and future, lie open to her divine vision."

"And Aztarky calls upon you here in your house?" Rowena prompted.

"*Astarte* first visited me in my dreams," said Madame

Sophonisba, "and then later in my waking hours. She revealed to me the great mission that lay in my future, that of enlightening the world with the flame of knowledge."

"Yes, the world is in sorry condition," Rowena agreed solemnly.

"One of the greatest secrets she has entrusted to me," the mystic continued, "is that we have all lived many times before, and the memory of those past lives can be reawakened."

"Oh, we have learned so much from Madame, thanks to the gift of Astarte," enthused lady Winderbrook. "She showed me that in ages past I was actually Guinevere, the bride of King Arthur. And in another life I was Anne of Cleves, one of the brides of Henry the Eighth."

"Most intriguing," said Rowena. "And you, Sir Murriot, you were also bride?"

Affronted at the suggestion, Sir Merriot's features suffused with a deep crimson. "Not a bit of it!" he barked. "I was once the noble Roman Marcus Brutus. In another century I was the Scottish king Macbeth." He stroked his whiskers in what he must have imagined was a very royal gesture. "Then again I was the famous Guy Fawkes."

It's interesting that they were always somebody famous, Artie thought, *never a kitchen maid or a chimney sweep.* It seemed as if the past lives revealed to them were intended to flatter their egos.

146

Rowena gave their hostess an inquiring look. "And knowing past lives gives benefit?"

"Why, yes," said Madame Sophonisba. "Those past lives greatly influence our present existence."

"It explains why I have remained unmarried in this life," chirped Lady Winderbrook. "After all, it is very difficult to find a man who could be a match for my previous husbands."

"Very hard," Rowena agreed. "Unless he is king."

"All of our lives form a continuous chain of destiny," Madame Sophonisba stated portentously.

"Yes, and destiny must be obeyed." Sir Merriot struck the arm of his chair decisively with his fist. "We must be guided by it or perish." He downed the last of his brandy in one swallow.

Rowena nodded sagely, as though thoroughly impressed by what she had heard.

"I believe from your letter of inquiry," prompted Madame Sophonisba, "that you are considering making a financial contribution to our great cause."

"I am not fool to spend money without sample of wares," Rowena cautioned her. "When might one have audience with this so wondrous Aztarky?"

Madame Sophonisba stood up and straightened out her skirts.

"Let us go and meet her now."

17.

The Temple of Astarte

Artie glanced over at his friend and saw that he had turned pale under his bushy wig. As they got up to follow the party, Ham whispered, "I don't like the sound of this, Artie. We might end up as a human sacrifice."

"Don't worry," Artie murmured back. "Rowena seems to have things well in hand."

"If you ask me," Ham muttered sourly, "she's having a little too much fun bossing us around."

They trailed along behind the group until Madame Sophonisba stopped in front of a set of double doors painted with images of serpents and lightning. She raised her arms above her head and stamped her left foot on the floor.

At once the doors swung inwards, as though opened by some unseen force. Craning forward, Artie caught a glimpse of a chamber painted in red and gold with a monstrous statue looming at the far end. Before he could manage a better look, Madame Sophonisba wheeled about and fixed him with a hostile glare.

"Servants are not permitted to desecrate this sacred space!" she declared in a voice that scraped his eardrums.

"Of course," Rowena agreed. "Temple is no place for buffoon."

"Send them to the kitchen," said Madame Sophonisba. "Perhaps cook can feed them some cabbage."

Rowena treated the boys to another stream of nonsense: "*Zborny falafel caboznotz dnavya! Popotkya kusko!*"

The boys retreated down the hallway, bowing as they went. Madame Sophonisba and her party entered the temple and the doors swung shut behind them.

"Rowena's pulling it off magnificently, isn't she?" said Artie.

"I suppose so," Ham conceded grudgingly. "But once we're out of here, she'd better get off her high horse."

"This is our chance to have a look around and see if we can find any trace of the dragon."

"I still wish we'd kept this business to ourselves," Ham grumbled, "instead of letting that awful girl stick her nose in."

From a door at the foot of the stairs wafted a smell of vegetables and the tuneless singing of the cook.

"That will be the kitchen," said Artie. "No point poking around in there."

Retreating, they peeked carefully through a few other doors but found only cupboards or ordinary rooms with nothing incriminating inside. Eventually they came to a flight of stairs leading downwards.

"They must go down to the cellar," guessed Artie. "I'll bet she's got some secrets stashed away down there."

The boys descended cautiously. At the foot of the steps was a short passage leading to a plain unpainted door.

"Probably just the coal cellar," Ham muttered.

"Shhh! I hear something," Artie whispered back.

He pressed his ear to the wooden panelling and listened to the voice on the other side. He couldn't make out what it was saying, but it wasn't talking in any normal way. It sounded like some sort of chant. Signalling Ham to keep quiet, he cautiously eased the door open.

In the room beyond, sitting with her back to them, was the maid who had greeted them at the door. Set into the wall in front of her were a number of brass levers and wheels. Unaware that she was being watched, the woman pulled a lever, turned a wheel and spoke into what looked like the bell of a trumpet.

"The veil of the future is parted before the all-seeing gaze of Astarte," she intoned.

Her voice was carried up a tube that penetrated the ceiling overhead. From above came the echo of her words, amplified by some acoustic device.

"Listen carefully, mortals, to my wisdom," the maid continued in the same deep tone.

Artie and Ham exchanged wide-eyed glances and backed away, gently closing the door after them. Once back upstairs, Ham asked, "What do you make of that then?"

"It's like the professor told me," Artie said. "Madame Sophonisba is a fake. She's got that servant of hers to imitate the voice of the goddess to fool those two disciples of hers."

"So she's not a real witch then?" The relief was obvious in Ham's face.

"She doesn't have any real mystical powers," said Artie. "She's just an unscrupulous fraud, but she does have a grudge against the professor, so she's still on our list of suspects. Come on, we'll explore upstairs."

They climbed stealthily to the upper floor. From below they could hear the muffled voice of Astarte still booming inside the temple.

The first door Artie tried led into a study decorated with potted plants and ivory statues. The wall to his right was covered in shelves stacked with leather-bound books. Ahead of him was a desk strewn with loose pages inscribed with strange symbols. He was moving in for a closer look when a horrid screech nearly made him jump out of his skin.

"Intruders in the temple! Intruders in the temple! Guards! Guards! Intruders in the temple!"

Wheeling about, Artie saw a brightly feathered parrot leap from its perch in a frenzy of rage. It swooped towards him and, as he threw up an arm to protect his face, its sharp claws ripped a tear in the sleeve of his Russian coat.

"Run!" he yelped, bundling Ham out the door.

They dashed back along the upstairs hall with the parrot shrieking in pursuit. "Traitors! Traitors! Off with their heads!"

Scrambling down the stairs, they were in such a rush that their feet became entangled. They tumbled down the last few steps and ended up in a groaning heap at the bottom. The parrot landed on the banister and squawked at them accusingly.

Artie struggled to recover his wits. When he looked up, Madame Sophonisba was standing over them with a dreadful scowl on her face.

"What is the meaning of this outrageous behaviour?" she demanded in a voice as harsh as the parrot's.

Artie scrambled to his feet and hauled Ham up beside him. While they stared stupidly and shook their heads, Rowena and the other two guests appeared behind Madame Sophonisba.

"Snooping about and thieving, eh?" growled Sir Merriot. "A sound horsewhipping is the answer to that."

152

"No whippings, please." Rowena raised a cautionary hand. "I question them." She fixed the boys with a scornful glare and treated them to a stream of interrogative gibberish.

"*Pizotna grosko deboyt? Vasni izpezni?*"

Artie realised he was supposed to respond. "Er… *gutbag follypot bin.*" He looked to his friend for support.

"*Follypot bin!*" Ham nodded his head emphatically.

Rowena turned to Madame Sophonisba. "They seek water closet to relieve bladder." She shook her head despairingly. "Is all I can do to stop them going in bushes."

"I will not have my property violated in this manner," said Madame Sophonisba. "You will see to their punishment, of course."

"Of course," Rowena agreed. "There will be great punishment with much squealing and gnashing of teeth. For now we make farewell."

With a departing nod to her hostess, she headed for the front door with the two boys trailing behind.

Once they were outside the gate Ham let out a huge gasp, as if he had been holding his breath until they reached safety.

"Well, that was a pretty rum business!" He climbed into the carriage.

"You don't know that half of it!" Rowena reverted to her normal voice. "You should have seen that temple."

Once they were all aboard, Mr Lampkin started his horse into motion without uttering a word.

"What was it like?" asked Artie.

"Well, there was a gruesome statue of this Astarte she's always talking about," said Rowena. "She has snakes for hair, a bird's beak for a nose and lots of fangs for teeth. I certainly wouldn't want to run into her when she's in a bad mood. Great clouds of incense came billowing out of her mouth. Honestly, the air was so thick with it I almost fainted."

"Did you learn anything?" Artie pressed her.

"Well, I learned that I used to be Catherine the Great, the empress of Russia," Rowena answered. "At least according to that ugly statue. It talks, you know."

"Yes, we know," said Ham.

Artie told her what they had discovered in the basement.

"That's a very saucy trick, I must say," said Rowena. "I rather suspected it was just a bit of flattery."

"What else did Astarte say?" Artie asked.

"Well, there was a lot of tosh about a new world dawning, the return of the ancient wisdom, that sort of thing. Then it said I was going to perform an act of generosity that would guarantee my future happiness."

"I suppose that means giving a lot of money to Madame Sophonisba to help her cause," said Artie.

154

"Cause indeed!" Rowena snorted. "I'll bet it all goes straight into her pocket."

"Well, she's certainly fooled that old chap with the red face and that little woman," said Ham. "They follow her around like she's the queen."

"So apart from falling downstairs, did you come up with anything else?" asked Rowena.

"We were about to search Madame Sophonisba's study when we were chased off by that vicious parrot," said Artie.

"Well, I don't think we're going to be welcomed back there," Rowena scratched at her wig delicately, "especially as I don't intend to give a penny to that frightful woman."

"But we now know for sure that the woman is a fake, with a grudge against the professor and experience in trickery and deception. That puts her firmly at the top of our list of suspects," Artie surmised.

Once they had changed out of their costumes at Rowena's house, she had Mr Lampkin drive the two boys home. Dropping them off at Sciennes Hill Place, the silent man doffed his hat and drove off.

"Do you think he even knows how to speak?" Artie wondered.

"There's hardly much point when that girl's around,"

said Ham. "She wouldn't let him get a word in edgewise."

They entered the tenement and climbed the stairs to the Doyle family flat. To Artie's surprise, Professor Anderson was there having tea with Mrs Doyle.

"The professor came by to see you, Artie," his mother explained. "He looked to me like he would be the better for a strong cup of tea. We've been discussing the exciting news about the Queen arriving in town today on her way to her annual holiday at Balmoral."

Artie could see that the tea was nearly black and Professor Anderson had barely touched it. He remembered how the professor had hoped to perform for Her Majesty. He was clearly depressed, but trying to put on a brave face.

Once they had finished their tea, Mrs Doyle gathered up the cups and teapot and carried them off to the kitchen. Only then did the Great Wizard reveal the reason for his visit.

"Mr Doyle, I wanted to hand you, your father and Mr Hamilton your last wages," he told them, "and to thank you personally for your efforts on my behalf. Unfortunately, without the dragon, I must cancel the show and let the Majestic return to its former state of abandonment."

"I suppose there's still no clue to how the robbery was committed?" inquired Ham.

"No." The magician shook his head sadly. "I'm afraid we just have to resign ourselves to the facts, impossible as they are."

As he clenched the money in his hand, Artie felt a fire growing inside him. They had been hired to help the professor and his show, and he was not giving up without a fight.

"No, professor, we're not beaten yet," he declared decisively. "Do you have the warehouse keys on you?"

"Yes, I carry them with me at all times. For all the use they are now."

"Good. We're going back to the scene of the crime. We're going to solve this mystery once and for all."

18.

Hocus Pocus

The warehouse was just as they had left it: empty except for a couple of work tables, a pair of stools and the ladder propped by the window. A gloomy atmosphere of desertion hung over the place. Once inside, Professor Anderson sank down on a stool with his elbows on his knees and his chin resting in the cup of his hand.

"I don't know why you brought us back here," Ham murmured as he followed Artie around the room. "You're just making the old fellow even more miserable."

"Ham, I know there's something we missed," Artie insisted. "We just have to think it through."

"Fine," Ham sighed. "What shall we think about?"

Artie set his jaw. "Well, for one thing, why did the robbers leave that ladder propped up under the window?"

"I suppose once they had what they came for, the

ladder was no use to them," Ham suggested, "so why not leave it behind?"

Artie climbed the ladder and peered out the window in both directions. Looking down at Ham, he said, "Why was the wagon just waiting there? The driver didn't make a move to leave until I raised the alarm."

"He could just be a dozy character who didn't have the sense to get out of here before somebody showed up."

"There's nothing dozy about this caper." Artie came back down. "So next we all ran off after the wagon."

"Yes, and when we caught up with it," Ham recalled, "it was empty and the driver had made off on his horse."

"We returned to the warehouse," Artie resumed, "but when we did, something was different."

Ham shrugged. "Not that I could see."

Still thinking, Artie stretched his arms out straight on both sides and slowly turned around, facing each of the four walls in turn. In his mind he tried to visualise the scene as it had appeared to him when they returned from the chase.

"That's it!" he exclaimed. "When we got back the place was larger!"

Ham gaped at him. "Artie, you're talking nonsense. Buildings don't grow larger or smaller in the space of five minutes."

"This one did." Artie hurried over to the window

and gazed to the right and left. "Ham, would you please light one of the lanterns on the table there and bring it here."

He moved the ladder over to the far left of the window. As soon as Ham handed him the lantern he climbed up and moved the light back and forth in the corner. Stretching his neck, he examined a spot just under the ceiling.

"There's some sort of mark," he observed. "It's like something scraped the wall up here."

"That might have been there for years," said Ham.

Professor Anderson suddenly sprang to his feet and Artie realised that he had been listening closely to them all along. The magician moved briskly around the room, his eyes darting this way and that. "Yes, of course, the ladder, the wagon, the chase, yes…"

"Artie, what have you done?" whispered Ham. "I think you've driven him over the brink."

"No, Ham, I think he's coming *back* from the brink."

Finally, the professor halted and a huge smile broke out across his face.

"You've hit the nail on the head, Mr Doyle," he enthused. "This wasn't a robbery at all. It was a magic trick!"

Soon they were racing across town in Professor Anderson's carriage. The magician chuckled to himself. "I was a fool not to have seen it."

"Artie, what is going on?" Ham looked perplexed. "I'm as much in the dark as ever."

Artie was beginning to understand. "It's all about how magic works. Half of the trick is that people only see what they expect to see."

"And the other half," the professor finished, "is misdirection."

When they arrived at the Alhambra Theatre the professor led them inside through the front doors. The staff were preparing everything for tonight's opening performance, and many of them clearly recognised the Great Wizard. No one made a move towards him as he strode purposefully down the passageway that led to the rooms backstage.

"So it was Kairos all along," Ham muttered aside to Artie.

"You heard the professor. It was a magic trick. Who else could have pulled it off?"

They came to a door with a large gold star painted on it. The professor knocked once then burst into the dressing room beyond. Louise and Kairos jumped up from where they had been seated.

"Yes, the two of you," said the professor. "I suspected as much."

"Father, please," said Louise, "I've been trying to—"

Kairos raised a hand to silence her. "No, Louise, let the Great Wizard speak his mind."

"Mr Doyle, Mr Hamilton," Professor Anderson said, "this is my errant son, Johnny."

"Er… yes," said Artie, "I did hear that you had a falling-out."

He thought it best not to let it slip that he had eavesdropped on the two of them.

"Young Johnny here thought he would do better to turn his back on his family and strike out on his own. He thought he could outmatch the Great Wizard, even to the extent of absconding with my magnificent dragon."

"Oh really?" his son challenged. "And how did I accomplish that?"

"It was very clever," the professor conceded, "and I didn't see through the trick until Mr Doyle here prompted me with a few insights."

Artie had formed a vague idea of how Kairos had spirited the dragon away. Now Professor Anderson outlined the theft in detail.

"First there was the misdirection," began the professor. "Why was the ladder left at the window? To draw our attention there as soon as we entered, so that we would be distracted from making a close examination of the warehouse interior."

"What good would that have done?" Ham queried. "The dragon was long gone."

"No, it wasn't," said Artie. "It was still there."

"Still there?" Ham was baffled. "Don't tell me it had turned invisible!"

"In a manner of speaking." The professor smiled thinly. "The thieves, presumably Johnny himself and some helpers, sawed through the bars during the night then climbed in through the window. They moved the crates from the centre of the room and placed them flush against the left-hand wall."

"But we could see the wall," Ham protested, "and there was nothing there."

"Remember the marks Mr Doyle found high up close to the ceiling?" the professor reminded him before turning to Artie. "What does that suggest to you, Mr Doyle?"

"Something was attached there that stretched the whole length of that wall?"

"Indeed," the professor nodded, "for our robbers had brought some equipment with them: a long pole, broken into sections, which they reassembled after passing it through the window. They fixed it up high and from this they hung a theatrical backdrop."

"Of course!" Artie exclaimed. "It was painted to look like a brick wall, matching the ones in the room. The crates were hidden behind it."

"But we would have noticed that, surely?" said Ham.

"Recall, Mr Hamilton, the dim morning light from the doorway and the small window," said Professor Anderson. "Our attention was centred on the empty space where the crates should have been."

"And as soon as we saw a ladder propped under the window," continued Artie, "we rushed straight there without looking anywhere else."

"Now look," Ham huffed, "this all sounds very fine, but it must be sheer bosh. Artie, when you looked out the window you saw the crates loaded up onto the wagon."

"Which is exactly what he was looking for," the professor explained, "and just what was needed to send us rushing out into the street to give chase."

"But they couldn't be in two places at the same time," Ham groaned, rubbing his forehead.

"What I saw on that wagon weren't the real crates." Artie now understood this for himself.

"An empty construct, probably made of cardboard, painted to look like a stack of wooden crates," the professor nodded.

Artie thought back to the scene. "That's why the wagon was empty when we caught up with it."

"Yes, the empty cardboard was collapsed into a flat package that could be carried off on horseback," said the professor.

"So what was all that chasing about for?" Ham asked.

"So the warehouse would be left empty with the doors wide open," Artie answered. He could see the younger magician nodding unconsciously in confirmation of their reconstruction.

"Some of Johnny's cohorts were keeping watch close by," the professor continued. "As soon as we were out of sight, they brought a second wagon in from a side street and rushed into the warehouse. They quickly dismantled the false wall then loaded it into the wagon along with the crates."

"By the time we got back from our wild goose chase they were gone," Artie finished. "It was a great help that they were stagehands and well used to moving props and scenery about in a hurry."

Johnny Anderson had been listening in silence and Artie could see that Louise was extremely nervous as they awaited their father's reaction. The professor gazed stonily at his son for a few moments, then his expression softened.

"I admit it, Johnny, that was one of the most ingenious tricks I have ever witnessed." He held out his hand.

Hesitantly, then with a smile, Johnny shook it. "I never intended to put a stop to your show," he apologised. "In fact I was going to return the dragon to you today."

"All Johnny wanted to do," Louise explained, "was to gain your respect as a magician in his own right."

"He's proved he is that." Professor Anderson gave his son an affectionate pat on the shoulder. "I was a fool to insist that you follow my path, Johnny. Please forgive a stubborn old man."

"There is only one Great Wizard," Johnny told him proudly, "and there will never be a greater, but I hope to be a well-respected Kairos."

The atmosphere in the room was one of happy relief. The professor was so delighted to have tracked down the missing dragon that he soon forgot the anxiety his son's trick had caused him.

"Alright," said Ham, "I think I've got the hang of all this hocus pocus now. But where exactly is the dragon?"

"It's right here, safe and sound, locked in the cellar. Come on, I'll show you." Johnny led the way down a flight of stairs with a key in one hand and a lantern in the other. "I'll have it transported to the Majestic for you."

"Good, good," said the professor. "There's still time to get everything ready for opening night."

When they reached the cellar door, Johnny pulled up abruptly and swallowed hard. Artie saw at once the reason for his shock. The lock had been smashed. The young magician gave the door a push and it creaked open to reveal an empty chamber beyond.

"Oh no, Artie," Ham gasped. "The dragon has vanished again!"

19.

Abracadabra

The Great Wizard staggered as though he had been struck across the face. Louise quickly took his arm to support him. Johnny Anderson appeared just as horrified by this turn of events and Artie felt sure this was not a further trick on his part.

"Who knew you had the dragon hidden down here?" Artie asked him.

"Only my stage crew," Johnny answered numbly, "and I would vouch for every one of them."

"I'm almost ready to accept that there is a curse at work," groaned Professor Anderson. He appeared completely crushed by this fresh disaster, not at all like the confident figure that had marched into the theatre only a short time ago.

Back upstairs they found a couch where the professor could lie down. Johnny went to fetch a sedative to settle his father's nerves and Artie took the opportunity to speak with Louise.

"It was you who came up with that extra invitation so your brother could attend the magic show," he surmised.

"Yes, I had a special one made," Louise confessed. "It was Johnny's own idea that it should be a joker. I've been trying to reconcile them for a long time, especially with Father coming out of retirement, and I thought it would help if he came to the show."

"But why did he come in disguise?" Ham asked.

"Johnny was concerned that if Father spotted him in the audience it would distract him," Louise explained. "A magician needs to maintain complete concentration when he's performing."

"In fact, the disguise made it doubly suspicious when he ran away after the explosion," said Artie.

"He was afraid that he would be suspected of causing the accident," said Louise, "on account of the bad feeling between the two of them – so he fled the scene."

"Are you quite sure he didn't do it?" asked Ham.

"Oh yes!" Louise was emphatic. "Johnny would never endanger anyone like that."

"No, he wouldn't," Artie agreed. Thinking out loud, he continued, "A skilled magician like him would have added just enough to the explosive mixture to spoil the trick without causing a fire."

"So whoever did it is completely ruthless then," Ham suggested.

"Or they haven't been trained in using magical materials like Johnny and Louise have," offered Artie.

Louise gazed sorrowfully at her father lying on the couch. Artie understood her pain only too well. He had seen his father stricken more often than he cared to remember.

"I don't know if we'll ever get to the bottom of this," Louise sighed.

Artie didn't want to admit it, but he was beginning to feel the same way. They only had two more days before the professor's show was to open.

The following day was a Sunday. As soon as he woke, Artie turned his mind to the case. He picked up his journal and out fell the note about Scobie's Lane.

IN SCOBIE'S LANE IS THE ANSWER WHICH ONE SEEKS

He pondered the note for a moment before starting a new entry in his journal.

The Case of the Vanishing Dragon

Suspects and clues:

- ~~Kairos~~ – no
- Madame Sophonisba – maybe, but we're not going back to investigate!
- Where is Scobie's Lane? Who could have left the note and why? Most likely one of the theatre staff?

After mass in the morning the Doyle family sat down to their Sunday lunch. Artie tried to raise the subject of Scobie's Lane, but his sisters kept interrupting, and Charles Doyle could only talk about the backdrops he had provided for the Great Wizard's show, which was to open the following night. Artie hadn't the heart to tell him that it had been cancelled. Finally, he managed to get his question in.

"Father, did you ever find out about Scobie's Lane?"

Charles Doyle let out a groan. "Artie, sometimes I swear my head is a sieve. I completely forgot about it. I will write myself a reminder to look into that as soon as I get to the office tomorrow."

"I'm sure that will be fine." Artie tried to hide his disappointment.

In the afternoon, Artie fetched Ham and they set out for Princes Street Gardens to meet Rowena. Ham was unhappy about the prospect of socialising with the Theatrical Phenomenon, even though she had promised them a picnic. Artie, however, was hopeful that she might help them shed some light on this increasingly murky mystery.

They met her at the gate of the West Gardens, where she had the boys unload a picnic hamper and blanket from Mr Lampkin's carriage before he drove off. The West Gardens were only open to people who had the money to pay an annual subscription, and it was obvious from the way the gatekeeper greeted her that Rowena was a regular visitor.

It was a bright sunny day and there was a holiday atmosphere because of the Queen's visit. Families were picnicking on the grass and in the midst of it all a brass band was playing a concert of patriotic tunes.

The three youngsters sat on a blanket and enjoyed their outdoor tea beneath the frowning crag of Edinburgh Castle. There were cheese sandwiches, strawberries and bottles of lemonade.

"You know, we could just be over in the East Gardens with the ordinary folk," Ham sulked. Artie knew he didn't like how Rowena flaunted her privilege.

"Oh no," Rowena objected, "over there it's all dust and din."

"That's because of all the work on the new bridge and rail station," said Artie. "Come on, Ham. Try a sandwich."

Ham made a start on the picnic and was soon munching happily, his pique forgotten.

"There's not much time to save the professor's show," said Artie. "It's supposed to open tomorrow night and I don't know where to start. I'm still no further forward with Scobie's Lane."

"What on earth is Scobie's Lane?" Rowena inquired.

"Somebody left Artie an anonymous note saying we'd find our answer there," Ham explained.

"Except it doesn't seem to exist," said Artie glumly.

"Probably just as well." Rowena nibbled on a strawberry. "It doesn't sound like the sort of place anybody would want to be seen."

"Magic is supposed to be all about smoke and mirrors," sighed Artie, "but so far all we have is a lot of smoke."

"It feels like we're stumbling about in the dark." Ham took a slurp of lemonade. "We still don't know who's been causing the accidents and we have no idea what's become of the dragon."

"It is a pretty pickle," agreed Rowena.

"Well, I don't think that Madame Sophonisba's off the hook yet," said Artie.

Ham nodded. "Anybody who's that greedy for money is capable of anything."

Rowena straightened. "It's probably never occurred to you two, but it isn't easy for a woman to make her own way in this world. A lot of avenues and careers are closed to us, and in many cases a woman has to marry somebody old and ugly just to have the means to live."

"You make it sound awful," Artie said quietly, somewhat abashed.

"And your life isn't exactly uncomfortable," Ham pointed out, somewhat less so.

Artie noticed a flash of resentment in Rowena's eyes but she limited her response to an irritated twitch of the mouth. "All I'm saying is that Madame Sophonisba has found a way to gain some status and wealth for herself. She may be dishonest, but perhaps no other alternative is open to her."

Artie was surprised to hear the girl expressing sympathy for someone else's circumstances. Perhaps there really was more to her than the vain creature she so often appeared to be.

"If money is her only motive," he said, "I don't see that she gains anything by trying to ruin the professor.

What do we know about those two disciples of hers?"

"Fortunately there's plenty of gossip in the circles I move in. Sir Merriot Ruthven lived abroad for many years before retiring to a manor house near Peebles. He owns a coal mine in Fife and I hear that he's rather too fond of indulging in brandy and opium."

"What about that little woman, Lady Winderbrook?" asked Ham.

"She's the sole heiress to her family's textile business, so she's pretty well off. There's a rumour that a few years ago a sea captain promised to marry her, then ran away with most of her jewellery and was never seen again."

Artie shook his head. "Even if we put them on the list of suspects, it's hard to see what they would get out of ruining the professor. It's hard to see what anybody would gain by it."

"I'm still not convinced Johnny and Louise are entirely innocent," said Ham. "Yes, they seem decent enough, but like you said, Artie, they're trained in the art of illusion."

"If we're going to go that far," said Artie, "then absolutely everybody is a suspect. Even us."

Ham pondered for a moment. "I say, you don't suppose the old boy has cooked all this up himself, do you – for publicity? You know, to create a big mystery around his new show like Sergeant McCorkle suspected?"

"If he did, he's turning in the greatest performance I've ever seen," replied Artie. "When we last saw him he appeared completely shattered by all these setbacks."

"He did say that even he's starting to believe he's cursed," said Ham.

"I think it's more likely the theatre's cursed," said Rowena. "I've heard stories about it being haunted."

"Yes, it could be that the ghosts are trying to scare everybody off," said Ham, "because they want the place all to themselves."

"That might explain the accidents," said Artie, "but ghosts could hardly steal the dragon from the Alhambra. I think you may be right about the theatre though. Perhaps it's all about the Majestic and not about the professor at all. Could there be something inside that somebody wants?"

"In that place?" said Rowena. "It's been closed for so long, if there was anything of value inside it would have been looted years ago."

"I suppose so," Artie conceded.

"Well, I've enjoyed the picnic," Ham polished off the last of the strawberries, "but we're no further forward. Every time we catch up with the dragon the blessed thing disappears."

Artie chewed his lip in frustration. "If only the key to the whole thing were as simple as a magic word, like *Abracadabra* or something."

When evening came, Mr Lampkin showed up in his carriage to drive them all home. First stop was Sciennes Hill Place. As Artie climbed down from the vehicle, he saw his father coming up the street towards him.

"Artie!" Mr Doyle hailed him. "Been out enjoying the summer sunshine, have you?"

"Sort of." Artie tried not to seem glum. He introduced Rowena and Mr Lampkin, and Mr Doyle greeted them all cheerily.

"Where have you been, Father?" Artie asked.

"Ah, well, I was feeling guilty about that favour you asked of me, so I let myself into the office and spent the afternoon rummaging through a lot of old maps."

Artie brightened up at once. "And did you find it?"

His father nodded and pulled a piece of folded paper from his pocket. "Scobie's Lane featured in one of the antique maps," he handed it to his son, "and I made this sketch for you."

Artie unfolded the paper and saw a network of streets marked out in his father's fine, detailed hand. "There are three or four streets here I've never heard of," he said.

"Yes, over the centuries," his father explained, "new streets were built on top of some of the old ones.

The old buildings were used as the foundations of the new. Are you coming up for tea?"

Artie was completely absorbed in studying the hand-drawn map. "Not right away. I think I have an errand to run first."

"Oh, well, cheerio then." Mr Doyle disappeared indoors.

Ham and Rowena got down from the carriage to look over Artie's shoulder at the map.

"What's so fascinating about this?" Rowena inquired.

"This is it!" Artie's heart was racing. "This is the key we've been looking for."

Ham stared at the paper and breathed, "*Abracadabra!*"

20.

Open Sesame

"I'm afraid I can't make head nor tail of this." Rowena squinted at the map. "It looks like a dreadful jumble."

"That's because my father has drawn in both the old streets," Artie explained, "and the new ones that have been built over them."

"Yes, there's Scobie's Lane." Ham pointed to where the name was clearly marked in Charles Doyle's precise script. "For the life of me, though, I can't see what use that is."

Artie frowned in concentration, running his finger across the map and visualising the layout of the Edinburgh streets in his mind as he knew them. "If I'm reckoning this correctly, it does all connect up. It looks to me like Scobie's Lane runs directly under the Majestic Theatre."

"What did that anonymous note of yours say again?" Rowena inquired.

"It said that's where we would find our answer." Artie could barely contain his excitement. "Now we know that it's hidden below the theatre!"

"So you think somebody wanted to stop Professor Anderson's show so that the Majestic would remain unoccupied?" said Ham.

Artie nodded vigorously. "Yes, so they could find their way down into Scobie's Lane without anybody knowing. Remember that before the professor and his people moved in, there were reports of strange lights and shadowy figures moving about the place?"

"Yes, ghosts," Ham recalled, turning slightly pale.

"Maybe not," said Artie. "Maybe that was somebody trying to get to Scobie's Lane."

"It's still a bit of a puzzle. What could they possibly want down there?" Rowena frowned. "I imagine it's pretty horrid after all these centuries."

"Perhaps," Ham suggested, "they've hidden the dragon down there."

"There's only one to way to find out," Artie decided. "We'll have to go and see for ourselves."

As Mr Lampkin drove them to the Majestic Theatre, the sinking sun cast long shadows over the streets. There were families wending their way home from their Sunday excursions and folk in carriages on their way to night-time appointments.

Artie could feel his pulse quickening as he reflected that the answer to the mystery might soon be within their grasp. Rowena's eyes sparkled with excitement, but Ham's head hung low as nibbled nervously on a bun he had saved from the picnic.

When they reached their destination Mr Lampkin dropped them off with a curt nod then left to pursue his own business.

"He's going to make a bit of extra money tonight," Rowena explained. "There's a big reception being held for the Queen at the City Chambers and lots of important people will be hiring cabs. He'll come back for us later."

How she knew all this Artie couldn't guess. He hadn't heard the cabbie speak a single word.

The front doors were securely locked, so they went around to the back to try the stage entrance, where they discovered that the lock had been broken.

"Well, somebody's definitely been here since the professor shut it down." Artie slowly pushed the door open.

They lit the lantern they had borrowed from Mr Lampkin and made their way cautiously down into the cellar, brushing cobwebs from their hair. The wooden steps creaked beneath their feet and Rowena flicked a spider from her sleeve.

"Well, this is quite the worst place I've been to in a long time," she complained.

"Hush!" Ham peered around anxiously. "You might wake up the ghosts."

Once they reached the bottom all they could see were planks, empty boxes and some old furniture, all of it covered in dust and grime.

"Well, I can't see a dragon," Ham whispered, "and it doesn't look like there's been any digging going on here." He waved the lantern about to illuminate all four corners of the room.

Artie continued to explore, examining an old wardrobe that was pressed against the wall. He got down on his hands and knees and peered at the cold stone floor.

"You're going to get filthy if you keep crawling around like that," Rowena cautioned him.

Artie ignored her. "Bring the light over here, Ham."

When Ham and Rowena joined him with the light Artie pointed to his discovery. "Look here. You can see a trail in the dust where the wardrobe has been moved back and forth."

"That means…" Rowena tapped a finger on her chin.

"There must be something behind it!" Artie concluded, jumping to his feet.

Together he and Ham heaved the wardrobe aside. As they did so, Rowena waved her hands in the air and called out, "Open sesame!"

"What are you on about?" Ham grunted.

"It's from the story of Aladdin," Rowena explained in a patronising tone. "It's what people say when they're opening a secret door. Honestly, what sort of a school do you go to?"

With a final push they cleared the wardrobe out of the way to expose a large hole in the wall.

"Somebody's taken a hammer to it and knocked the bricks out." Artie pointed to the gap. "That's the way into Scobie's Lane."

Ham drew back a step. "Remember, Artie, we still don't know who left you that note. They might have done it to lure us into a trap."

Artie shook his head. "No, I'm sure somebody wanted to leave us a clue without giving herself away."

"Herself?" echoed Rowena. "You think you know who it is then?"

"I've got a pretty good idea." Artie peered down the gaping hole. "Come on."

He took the lantern and led the way into the darkness beyond.

They descended a short earthen slope and gathered together while Artie hoisted the lantern as high as his arm would go. Stretching off into the darkness before them was Scobie's Lane.

Grey walls pitted with age rose up on both sides, with rotted shutters hanging from their empty windows.

Battered doors had fallen into the street and broken bricks and beams littered the ground. It was hard to imagine that living people had ever occupied this dismal subterranean world, or that it had ever seen the light of day.

"This place is about as cheery as a graveyard," muttered Ham.

Rowena shuddered and Artie nodded in agreement.

The three visitors walked slowly up the lane, grit and broken mortar crunching softly under their feet. The gloom was so intense it was impossible to tell how far the buried street stretched away before them. Every step seemed to take them deeper and deeper into a ghostly realm where they might easily be lost forever.

"Look how a path has been cleared through the rubble," Artie pointed out. Loose piles of stone, earth and sand were banked up against the walls on either side. "It must have been done fairly recently.

"But what on earth is the point?" said Ham. "Why would anyone want to venture down here?"

Rowena clamped a hand across her mouth to stifle a squeal as a rat scampered across their path. "What a frightful place! Artie, are you sure we're safe?"

Artie glanced up and saw that wooden supports had been hammered into place to keep the roof from crumbling.

"It all looks pretty solid," he said. "As if this structure has been built by someone who's experienced at working below ground."

They continued their progress, staring at the empty doorways and windows, hoping no faces would gaze back. They came upon some discarded tools, picks and shovels that had been used to clear the route through the rubble-strewn street, as well as ropes for hoisting up timbers and hauling large chunks of masonry out of the way.

"It's so stuffy down here," Rowena pinched her nose, "and the smell is just awful."

"There's a dead end up ahead." Ham peered into the gloom. "I can't say I'll be sorry to turn around and head back."

Scobie's Lane ended in a solid wall of earth. Packed against it, heaped up row upon row, was an array of small barrels.

"What's in those kegs, I wonder?" said Rowena. "Wine?"

Artie pressed his nose close to one of the barrels and sniffed. "No, not wine. I know that smell. It's gunpowder!"

"Gunpowder?" echoed Rowena. "What's it doing down here?"

"Look!" Artie pointed at the lengths of cord trailing from the barrels. "The fuses are set and ready to be lit!"

Ham recoiled a pace. "Why would anyone want to blow up this old place?"

"It certainly wouldn't be much of a loss," Rowena muttered.

Artie pulled out his father's sketch map and examined it by the light of the lantern. As he did so an awful realisation dawned on him. "It's not Scobie's Lane they want to destroy. We're directly under the City Chambers."

Rowena's eyes widened in horror. "But that's where they're holding the reception for the Queen right now."

Ham gaped at the wall of powder kegs. "If this lot goes off…"

"It will blow the foundations out of the City Chambers." Artie's voice was grim. "The building will collapse in ruins, killing everybody inside. Including Queen Victoria."

21.

Vanishing Act

"So this whole thing has been a plot to kill the Queen." Rowena stared upward as though she could see through to the glittering event taking place far above their heads: the music, the champagne and the Queen surrounded by Edinburgh's most notable figures. "How dreadful! But who would want to do such a thing?"

"I can think of someone," said Artie. "Sir Merriot Ruthven."

"What, that old codger we saw at Madame Sophonisba's?" asked Ham. "What has he got against the Queen?"

"He thinks that in a former life he was Guy Fawkes," explained Artie, "one of the conspirators who tried to blow up the Houses of Parliament. What people often forget is that their aim was to kill the king who was inside at the time."

"He also believes he was Marcus Brutus, one of the men who murdered Julius Caesar, the ruler of Rome," Rowena reminded them. "And Macbeth, who only became king of Scotland after murdering King Duncan. I know because I was once in that play about him."

"We heard Sir Merriot say that destiny has to be obeyed," said Artie. "He thinks it's his destiny to murder the monarch because that was what he did in his previous lives."

"Artie, do you know what this means?" Ham was appalled. "It means we've got to get out of here before he comes back – he's a complete lunatic!"

"And a very dangerous one," said Artie as they backed away from the gunpowder kegs.

"Sadly, that is true," came a voice out of the darkness.

They spun round to see a girl's pale face floating in the air towards them.

"A ghost!" yelped Ham, staggering backwards.

"No, Ham, it's not a ghost." Artie grabbed his friend's arm to steady him. "It's Delphine."

As the Frenchwoman drew closer, they saw she was wearing a long-sleeved black dress so that only her face was illuminated by the candle she was holding.

"Delphine, what are you doing here?" Rowena demanded. "Surely you're not responsible for all of this?"

"No, she isn't," said Artie. "She's involved, but she did try to warn us with that note."

"It is true," Delphine agreed. "And it did lead you here."

"You suspected her already, Artie." Ham looked at his friend. "But how?"

"That message she left me: *In Scobie's Lane is the answer which one seeks.* That's a very odd way of putting it in English – *which one seeks* – but it's very natural in French. She's the one who's been causing the accidents."

Ham was aghast. "But why, Delphine? Why would you help that madman?"

"Was it money?" Rowena suggested. "Or blackmail?"

"Neither of those." Delphine shook her head miserably. "It is because he is my father."

"Look, we should get out of here," said Artie, leading the way back up Scobie's Lane. "You can tell us all about it on the way, Delphine."

The French girl took a deep breath to steady herself, then began her tale as they walked.

"I grew up in Paris with no knowledge of my father. Only when my dear mama died the year past did I find a letter telling me he was a rich man named Sir Merriot Ruthven. I had nowhere to live and could find no work, so I tracked him to his house here in Scotland, in the hope he would accept me as his daughter. He was sometimes kind, sometimes cross that I had appeared at all. When he asked me to do him a favour, I saw it as a chance to win his affection."

"Yes, I suppose that's understandable," said Rowena sympathetically.

"He asked you to join the company Professor Anderson was putting together," guessed Artie.

"That is so. He felt that because I was pretty and could sing and dance, I would be given a part in the show. He was correct, and I enjoyed my work. Then he asked me to stage one or two small accidents during the rehearsals. They were little things and I said yes to please him. But I made a mistake with the explosive mix that night at the Pantheon Theatre. Poor Laurence might have been killed."

"That frightened you into ceasing your sabotage," Artie surmised.

Delphine shuddered. "I was afraid someone might be badly hurt. I explained this to Sir Merriot and he became angry. He had been drinking and spoke of Scobie's Lane and how he needed to get there."

"I don't understand, Delphine," Ham shook his head. "You were the victim of one of those so-called accidents."

"She caused it herself," said Artie. "I expect she had a small blade concealed in her hand and used that to cut the cord."

"Yes, to please Sir Merriot I had to cause another accident, and the only way to avoid endangering anyone else was to make myself the victim."

"But because you were ready for the fall," said Artie, "you were able to avoid serious injury."

"Even so, my father was not satisfied, so in order to stop another of his rages I had to find another way for him to interfere in Professor Anderson's plans."

"You told him about the mechanical dragon," said Artie.

Delphine nodded sadly. "Yes, we all knew it was being constructed somewhere. Sir Merriot had the professor followed to find where it was stored, and he set a man to watch the place at all hours."

"That was how he knew the dragon had been stolen and taken to the Alhambra Theatre." Artie was seeing it all clearly now. "His man followed Johnny Anderson there when he was making off with it. During the night Sir Merriot and his henchmen broke in and stole it."

"And with the show closed down, he would have the Majestic Theatre to himself again," said Ham.

"He must have read about the plans for the Queen's reception weeks ago," said Artie. "Somehow he knew about Scobie's Lane and he devised this assassination plot. I would guess he brought in some experienced men from his coal mine to break through the wall and clear a path."

Rowena was fanning herself with her hand. "Really," she moaned, "the air in here is so thick and smelly. Oh dear, look at the state of my dress." She stopped and began brushing the dust from her clothes with her hands.

Artie continued his explanation. "Professor Anderson ruined things by reopening the theatre and Sir Merriot couldn't complete his job while people were working here day and night preparing the place for the professor's big show."

Ham was staring at the dancer in frank dismay. "But, Delphine, how could you be party to anything so heinous?"

"I did not know what he wanted with this Scobie's Lane," said Delphine. "I left you that message in hope that you would uncover the truth, Artie. Tonight I finally dared to look for myself and found the way down here already open."

"Yes, thanks to us," said Ham.

"Until I overheard you talking, I did not realise what an atrocity he had in mind." Delphine glanced anxiously back down the lane towards the deadly supply of gunpowder.

"Look, there's the way out up ahead," said Artie.

Delphine began to hurry. "Good. We must inform the police at once."

"It's a little late for that now, you stupid girl!"

The harsh words were accompanied by the menacing sound of a pistol being cocked. Sir Merriot Ruthven was coming down the earthen slope towards them with a gun in his right hand. In the other he held a lantern by the light of which they could see the dreadful grin on his red, leering face.

"Heaven help us!" breathed Ham.

Artie raised his hands in surrender. "Sir Merriot, please, stop this now. Nobody's been hurt yet. It's not too late to abandon this mad scheme."

"Quiet!" Sir Merriot snapped. "I'll stand for no more of you insolent whelps and your confounded interference. Back up the tunnel, all of you!"

As he herded them back into the darkness, Artie was aware that Rowena had disappeared. There was every chance Sir Ruthven hadn't seen her.

"Oh, Father," pleaded Delphine, "think of all those poor people up there."

"I'll have no whining out of you either," her father sneered. "You've played your part and now I'm done with you."

Soon they were once again face to face with the dreadful array of explosives. Sir Merriot waved them back from the wall and aimed his pistol at them menacingly.

"Now, down on your bellies!"

They lay down flat and Artie felt the rough, gritty surface grating against his cheek.

"One move, just one," their captor warned, "and it's a bullet for each of you."

All three of them lay helplessly while Sir Merriot fetched some rope. Quickly and roughly he tied their wrists behind their backs and bound their ankles together. With his prisoners secured, he pocketed his revolver and began twisting the fuse wires together into a single master fuse.

"Artie, where's Rowena gone?" Ham whispered.

"Shhh!" Artie hushed him, afraid the madman might overhear.

"What's that?" snapped Sir Merriot, turning at the sound of their voices.

"We were just wondering," said Artie, "about Madame Sophonisba coming to the theatre to threaten Professor Anderson. What made her do that?"

"I goaded her into it," Sir Merriot growled, "by reminding her of the wrongs he had done her. I hoped her dire warnings would drive his crew away."

"So she was duped," said Artie, "just like the miners you brought down here to dig a way through."

Sir Merriot gave a throaty chuckle as he completed the master fuse. "Those idiots! They think we're going to blast our way into a bank vault and they're eager for a share of the loot. They have no idea what's actually up there. What a shock they'll get when they read about it in the papers tomorrow."

He took out some matches, struck one and lit the master fuse. Then he fetched an empty wooden box and sat down on it, gazing about him with the satisfaction of a job well done.

"About five minutes that will take," he said as the fuse sputtered and smoked.

Delphine let out a despairing moan and Ham muttered, "Maybe this detective business was a bad idea after all."

"Sir Merriot, listen." Artie struggled to speak calmly. "When those miners learn what you've done, they'll lead the police straight to you."

Their captor slipped a silver flask from his pocket and took a long swallow of brandy. "Let 'em," he croaked. "They'll find me right here, buried along with you three and all those revellers up there." He jerked a thumb in the direction of the building overhead.

"You mean you're staying here?" Ham squeaked.

"To the end." Sir Merriot took another swig from the flask, as though toasting himself.

"But, Father, you'll be killed," sobbed Delphine.

"Don't you understand?" he crooned with an insane gleam in his eyes. "That doesn't matter. I'm going to be reborn into another life. I'll be a king once more, perhaps even an emperor, ruler of half the world."

His harsh laughter echoed mockingly around them as the tiny flame continued its way along the fuse wire towards the waiting gunpowder.

22.

The Phantom Voice

In an agony of despair Ham tried to wriggle his way loose of the ropes that bound him.

Sir Merriot immediately drew his pistol. "Keep still, drat you!" he snarled. "Any more of that and I'll finish you right now."

Ham gave up his struggle and turned away from the madman, not wanting to show his tear-stained face.

Artie's heart was pounding like a hammer against his chest. He stared at Sir Merriot, appalled by the realisation that it was impossible to reason with a man who had lost all sanity. He wondered what had become of Rowena. If she was sneaking to the surface to fetch help, they would never get here in time. In a matter of minutes they would all be destroyed in a catastrophic explosion.

Sir Merriot laid the pistol down at his side, keeping it within easy reach in case he should be provoked again.

He was taking another gulp of brandy when a high, ethereal voice came to him out of the darkness.

"Macbeth, Thane of Glamis, Thane of Cawdor, King to be!"

Ruthven sprang to his feet, the flask dropping from his startled fingers to clatter on the ground.

"Who's there?" he challenged, snatching up his pistol. "Show yourself, whoever you are!"

"Macbeth, husband," came the eerie voice, "it is I, your wife, Lady Macbeth, come to join you in your hour of triumph."

"Wife?" Sir Merriot echoed. "My lady?"

"Yes, my love, it is I," crooned the voice. "Remember how we schemed to do away with King Duncan, how I helped you to seize the throne?"

Ruthven's eyes glazed over, as if he had wandered into a dream. "Yes, I remember… There was blood, so much blood."

"Yes," said the voice, "too much to ever wash away. But I have a vision of your future. Come follow and I will show it to you."

"Follow?" Sir Merriot looked around in confusion.

"It is not far. The veil of time has opened for me, and I can lift the curtain if you will but follow my voice."

The crazed nobleman gazed yearningly into the blackness and picked up his lantern. With stumbling steps he followed the ghostly voice back up Scobie's Lane. As the light dwindled into the distance Ham gasped, "Artie, he's gone! What do we do now?"

Artie turned and by the light of the remaining lantern saw a flicker of hope in his friend's wet and grimy face.

"Just give me a moment," he answered. "The professor taught me a rather useful trick." While Sir Merriot was tying his wrists, he had flexed them as Professor Anderson had instructed, so that when he relaxed them again there would be some slack to play with. Now he used that to work free of the loops.

"That voice," said Delphine, "came from where?"

"It's Rowena," explained Artie. "It turns out she is a very talented actress."

With a grunt he yanked one hand free, feeling some of his skin scrape off on the rough rope. He cast aside the bonds, untied his ankles, then made a dive for the burning fuse. He beat at it with the flat of his hand but the flame would not die. Jumping to his feet he stamped on it again and again until at last it was snuffed out with only inches to spare.

He quickly released the other two, then began tugging the fuse wire out of the powder kegs.

"Come and help me!" he urged. "If we don't pull out the fuses, Sir Merriot could come back at any moment and light them again."

With Ham and Delphine's help, he gathered up all the fuse wire into a ball and flung it into the dark interior of one of the hollow houses.

"How long do you think Rowena can keep leading him on?" asked Ham. "I know he's cracked, but sooner or later he's bound to discover that it's a trick."

Artie snatched up their lantern and led the way along Scobie's Lane. "Let's hope we catch up with her before he does."

Hurriedly retracing their steps, they climbed back up into the theatre.

"Delphine, you go and fetch the police," Artie instructed. "Get them here as fast as you can."

"Yes, yes." Delphine dashed to the open stage door.

"Where to now, Artie?" asked Ham.

"Knowing Rowena as we do, there's one obvious place to look," Artie guessed.

They hurried down the passageway and started up the steps to the stage. As they did so, a row of gas jets flared into life to illuminate the scene. Sir Merriot stood at the far end, where he had activated the lights. Now clearly visible, Rowena was crouching ineffectually behind an artificial palm tree.

"Husband! Macbeth! Do you not know me?" she pleaded as he strode angrily towards her, brandishing his revolver.

"Drat and damnation!" he swore. "I'll have your hide for this, girl! No more of your confounded tricks!"

He grabbed her by the wrist, hauled her out of hiding and flung her violently to the floor. "I'll not be trifled with, do you hear?"

Artie bounded onto the stage. "Leave her alone, you brute!" he yelled.

"You!" roared Sir Merriot, his eyes ablaze with furious hate. "Am I never to be rid of you brats?"

"Artie, look out!" Ham shrieked as the madman aimed his pistol.

He hurled himself onto his friend and they both crashed to the floor as a bullet streaked over their heads to smack into the plaster wall.

Rowena scrambled across the stage to join the boys as the crazed nobleman took fresh aim.

"I'll be done with all of you," he raved, "then I'll blow the gunpowder! Destiny cannot be denied!"

Suddenly his finger froze on the trigger and his body was shaken by a horrid convulsion. "No, no!" he gasped. "You cannot come for me now…"

Artie realised he was staring past them into the darkness beyond the stage.

"I know you have haunted this place since the fire." The madman's voice was harsh and laboured. He waved his pistol this way and that, as if trying to hold an unseen enemy at bay. "But you cannot take me now! It's not my destiny!"

He staggered backwards, retreating from the invisible horror.

In a flash Artie realised that the maniac was directly beneath one of the scenic backdrops suspended from the rafters overhead. With only an instant to seize this advantage, he lunged for the rope that held it secure. He swiftly loosed it from the bracket where it was tied and down came the scenery.

Sir Merriot flailed at his invisible tormentors as the backdrop, weighted along the bottom by a long wooden pole, came crashing down and knocked him unconscious to the floor.

Only then did Artie see that it was the painted background to the dragon's cave, a wall of yellow stone veined with silver and studded with emeralds and rubies. Below it Sir Merriot lay pinned, the pistol lying just beyond his outstretched arm.

For a moment the silence was almost overwhelming. Then Rowena let out a cry of joy and relief.

"Oh, Artie, I so hoped that if I lured him away you would find a way to free yourselves."

Standing up, they gathered around the unconscious nobleman. Artie picked up the pistol and smiled at the girl.

201

"That was a very brave thing you did, Rowena."

"And quite a performance," Ham admitted. "Artie, do you think…" He gazed anxiously about the stage. "Do you think he actually saw… ghosts?"

Artie stared down at the insensible villain with a mixture of disgust and pity. "Ham, that's a mystery that will have to wait for another day."

23.

Opening Night

By the time Sir Merriot Ruthven began to stir, Delphine had returned with Professor Anderson, Sergeant McCorkle and a pair of constables. She had found the Great Wizard at the police office making a last desperate appeal for them to take the theft of the dragon seriously and organise a search while there was still time to rescue the show.

Artie handed the pistol to McCorkle and stood aside as the constables took hold of Ruthven and hauled him to his feet.

"This young woman has been telling me a fantastic tale about a plot to blow up the Queen." McCorkle thrust the gun into the pocket of his long coat.

"It's true, sergeant," said Artie. "If you go down to the cellar you'll find an underground passage with all the evidence you need."

"It is a remarkable story, that's for sure," McCorkle stroked his moustache, "but if there is evidence, as you say, then it must be the truth. Facts do not lie. However," he added warningly, "I must caution you to speak to no one of this until we have carried out a thorough investigation."

"Of course, sergeant, I understand." Artie nodded.

Ham and Rowena also added their agreement.

"And if you search Sir Merriot's estate," said Artie, "I'm sure you'll find the stolen dragon."

"Oh, I do hope so," breathed Professor Anderson. "We may be able to save the show in time for tomorrow's opening night."

"It is a sorry state of affairs," McCorkle frowned at Sir Merriot, "when a noble of the realm engages in such low skulduggery and black-hearted treason."

Ruthven made no answer, but stumbled off groggily, pinned between the two policemen. He was mumbling to himself but no one could make any sense of what he was saying. Once he was out of sight, McCorkle turned back to the youngsters.

"Well now, Master Doyle, it appears you have got yourself into another of your scrapes and then cleverly extricated yourself."

"Yes, with a bit of luck," said Artie, "and a lot of help from my friends."

McCorkle unhooked a lantern from his belt. "And now I had best proceed to examine the scene of the crime, this subterranean passage you have spoken of."

"I will show you the way, monsieur." Delphine led the policeman backstage.

"Mr Doyle, Mr Hamilton, Miss McCleary," Professor Anderson nodded to each of them in turn, "I can barely express my gratitude for all you have done."

"You were paying us to do a job, sir," said Artie. "I'm just glad we succeeded."

"Of course," added Ham, "we wouldn't say no to a bonus. Perhaps a really good supper?"

"That is the least I can do." The Great Wizard grinned. "And what about you, Miss McCleary, how can I reward you?"

"I was thinking," Rowena rose up on her toes, "that as well as my song, I might be permitted to dance."

Artie spotted that Ham was about to groan, and silenced him with a jab in the ribs.

Anderson smiled broadly. "I am sure that can be accommodated also."

The next evening, as Artie and Ham took their seats for the opening night of *The Princess and the Dragon*, it was still hard to believe how close they had come to utter disaster. Instead of the whole city being in mourning for a catastrophic loss of life and the murder of the beloved Queen, all the news was of a successful royal visit.

A search of Sir Merriot Ruthven's estate had uncovered the stolen dragon hidden away in his stables. The whole crew worked overtime to ensure that the show opened on schedule in the newly refurbished Majestic Theatre.

Artie and Ham, along with their families, had been given exclusive front-row seats. Artie could see how proud his father was to find his name featured in the programme, and he was dressed in his best suit for the occasion. His mother, too, in her evening finery, might well be taken for visiting royalty, Artie reflected with a smile. Artie was also pleased to see Johnny Anderson in the audience. Now that they had overcome their disagreements, father and son were discussing the possibility of going on tour together.

When Miss Clatter learned of what Rowena had been through, she insisted the girl rest in bed and fussed over her terribly. Rowena was adamant, however, that she had suffered no ill effects from the ordeal and that she would perform her song as originally planned.

As everyone now knew, the climax of the show would be the astonishing illusion of *The Princess and the Dragon*. Delphine retained the role of the princess, as no charges had been brought against her. In fact,

Professor Anderson had taken her under his wing almost as a true father would.

While they were waiting for the house lights to dim, Ham wondered, "So what's going to become of that madman, Sir Merriot?"

"The doctors have judged him to be completely insane," said Artie, "so there will be no trial. In fact, the whole thing has been hushed up, in the public interest, as they say."

"You'd think we'd get some credit for saving the day," Ham groused.

"You could always write the story up yourself," Artie suggested jokingly.

Ham made a disgruntled face. "I'm giving up on that writing lark. It's just too hard trying to think of all the words. Also I'm sick of getting ink all over my fingers. No, I'll leave that to you and concentrate on detective work."

There was a buzz of anticipation as the orchestra struck up a theme from Mozart's *The Magic Flute* and the house lights began to dim. Artie heard Ham's mother give an excited squeak. The curtain began to rise and the theatre resounded with excited applause.

Soon the stage was a scene of continual wonder as the Great Wizard conjured flowers, birds and animals out of the air, vanished volunteers from the audience and made Louise float above the stage on a bed of flowers.

In the intervals between his magical illusions there were jugglers, acrobats and fire-eaters. Delphine performed an Arabian dance to huge applause, and then Rowena skipped onto the stage to sing:

"Mid pleasures and palaces though we may roam
Be it ever so humble, there's no place like home.
A charm from the skies seem to hallow us there
Which seek through the world, is ne'er met elsewhere.
Home! Home! Sweet, sweet home!
There's no place like home, there's no place like home."

There was a heartfelt longing in Rowena's voice that Artie found very moving. It was as though she were singing to her absent parents, calling them back from their endless foreign travels.

"An exile from home splendour dazzles in vain.
Oh give me my lowly thatched cottage again,
The birds singing gaily that came at my call
And gave me the peace of mind dearer than all.
Home! Home! Sweet, sweet home!
There's no place like home, there's no place like home."

At the close of the song she performed a short, balletic dance, which, though not as agile as Delphine, she carried out gracefully. At the end she clasped her hands to her heart, gazing heavenward in a pose that invited applause.

There were plenty of cheers, which prompted Rowena to bow repeatedly with a beaming smile on her face.

"Actually," Artie joined in the applause, "she's not half bad."

"I suppose not," Ham agreed grudgingly. "But in future we don't want that girl interfering in our cases."

"She has a name, you know," said Artie. "You could call her Rowena."

"No, Artie," said Ham with a decisive shake of the head. "To me she will always be *that girl.*"

Finally Rowena left the stage, throwing kisses to the audience as she went. Now it was time for the grand finale – the tale of *The Princess and the Dragon.*

Professor Anderson appeared on the stage in the colourful robes and turban of an oriental wizard. "And now," he announced, "a magical tale from ancient China, brought to life before your very eyes."

He narrated the action while the orchestra provided a dramatic accompaniment, telling the audience about the great dragon that terrorised the Chinese kingdom.

The curtain was raised to reveal the magnificent monster in all its glory. The dragon flapped its wings and roared, flames spouting from its jaws. There were gasps from the audience, and for a moment Mrs Doyle covered her eyes in shock at the sight.

Delphine appeared in the silk gown of a Chinese princess. The Great Wizard explained that to persuade the dragon not to destroy the kingdom, the princess had to be given as a sacrifice. Delphine performed a dance that expressed both sorrow and fear before turning to face the dragon with a courage that brought cheers from the audience.

The Great Wizard promised that his magic would keep her safe, even if the dragon devoured her. With a last pathetic glance at the audience, Delphine stepped into the dragon's lair. The monster reached out its claws, opened wide its jaws and belched out a cloud of smoke which quickly covered the entire stage.

A huge roar shook the theatre and the cloud dispersed to show that the dragon and the princess had vanished.

"Behold!" cried the Great Wizard, pointing upward. "The beast flies off with its prey!"

All eyes turned upward to see the dragon, wreathed in a great white cloud, flying over the heads of the audience.

"I promised the princess she would be safe!" Professor Anderson declared.

As he spoke he hurled a handful of sparkling dust into the air, whereupon the dragon burst into flame and disappeared in a billow of smoke. There were gasps and squeals, and then, to the delight of the crowd, Delphine descended out of the blazing cloud like a delicate angel, sliding down a long, silken cord.

She landed lightly upon her feet right in the midst of the astonished audience, who burst into almost deafening applause. Like everyone else, Artie clapped and cheered, his eyes wide with wonder. With his magnificent performance, the Great Wizard had demonstrated to one and all that nothing – absolutely nothing – was impossible.

Artie realised now that he was no longer worried about the rest of his life. He knew that the future, with all its promise, would come in its own good time. Just like magic.

Author's Note

Spoiler alert! Do not read this without reading the book first!

Throughout his life, Arthur Conan Doyle, the creator of Sherlock Holmes, had a strong interest in the supernatural, and for many years he was good friends with the famous magician and escape artist Harry Houdini.

John Henry Anderson, born in Kincardineshire in 1814, began performing magic at the age of seventeen. He became famous throughout the world as the Great Wizard of the North, performing his tricks and illusions across America and Russia, where he was a great favourite of the Tsar. He was assisted in his performances by his daughter Louise and had a serious falling-out with his son Johnny when the young man left the family to launch a magical career of his own.

Scobie's Lane is my invention, but Edinburgh does have real underground streets. The most famous is Mary King's Close, which is now open as a tourist attraction. In 1872 there were two unsuccessful attempts to kill Queen Victoria. In each case the would-be assassin was judged to be insane.

As well as investigating some of the true history behind this story, you can also see how Sherlock Holmes solves equally baffling mysteries in stories like *The Red-Headed League* and *The Speckled Band* by Sir Arthur Conan Doyle.

For more on *The Artie Conan Doyle Mysteries* and my other projects, visit my website: www.harris-authors.com

Robert J. Harris

"So the mystery of the Vanishing Dragon has been solved," said Ham. "Whatever shall we do next?"

"Well," replied Artie, "I daresay another mystery will present itself in due course..."

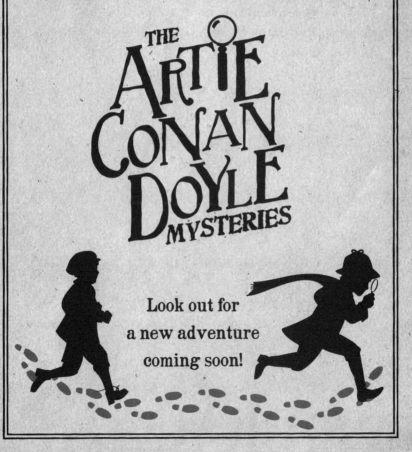

THE ARTIE CONAN DOYLE MYSTERIES

Look out for
a new adventure
coming soon!

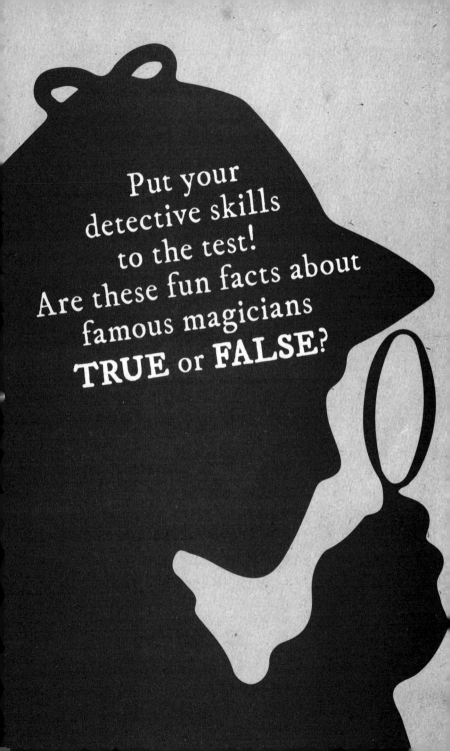

Put your
detective skills
to the test!
Are these fun facts about
famous magicians
TRUE or **FALSE?**

1. John Henry Anderson was given his stage name — the Great Wizard of the North — by famous Scottish author Sir Walter Scott.

2. John Henry Anderson was the first magician to pull a rabbit out of a top hat live on stage.

3. Sir Arthur Conan Doyle was good friends with magician Harry Houdini, until they disagreed over the existence of real psychics.

4. Houdini once made a rhinocerous disappear live on stage in New York.

5. Dynamo, one of the most famous modern magicians, once walked on water across the River Clyde in Glasgow.

1 True 2 True 3 True 4 False, it was an elephant
5 False, it was the River Thames in London

Looking for another mystery?
Read on for an exciting extract from:

Artie Conan Doyle
and the Gravediggers' Club

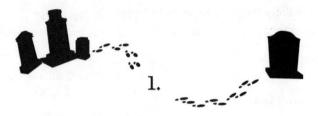

1.

The Adventure of the
Haunted Graveyard

Edinburgh, January, 1872

As the winter's night fell, an icy sea fog crept over Leith then nosed its way up the narrow streets and alleyways of Old Edinburgh. It spread silently over Greyfriars Kirkyard, washing up against the walls of the church and coiling about the trees and gravestones. A distant clock struck ten as two figures, a pair of twelve-year-old boys, made their way cautiously through the murk.

"*Arthur Conan Doyle*," declared Artie Doyle. "That's what it will say on my tombstone, Ham, my full and proper name. And underneath that it will say, *He achieved greatness as… as…*"

"As what, Artie?" asked his friend Edward Hamilton.

"I don't know yet, Ham," Artie confessed. "That will take a bit of finding out."

Ham's green plaid jacket was buttoned right up to the neck, his shoulders hunched against the cold.

"I do wish you wouldn't talk about being dead." He tugged his cap down over his ears. "I've got goosebumps already just from sneaking around this graveyard."

Artie was also dressed for a winter's night in a tweed jacket, knee-length woollen trousers, long thick socks and a pair of stout leather boots. He tightened his scarf as he walked among the gravestones.

"Don't complain," he chided his friend. "Getting in here turned out to be easier than I thought, what with the lock on the gate being broken."

"A good thing too," said Ham. "I'd likely have ripped my britches climbing over it."

Artie stopped and rubbed his hands together. "Doesn't that broken lock suggest something to you?"

"It suggests to me that the watchman has been sleeping on the job."

"That's true, I suppose," Artie agreed. "But to me it suggests somebody wanted access to the kirkyard after hours. I wonder how long the lock has been broken."

"It may not mean anything." Ham jammed his hands deep into his pockets. "It might have been damaged by accident."

Artie frowned at his friend. "Look, there's no point sneaking out of the house in the middle of the night to have an adventure if you keep saying everything's an accident or a coincidence."

Ham gave a huff. "I'm sure I didn't mean to spoil it for you."

A shaft of moonlight suddenly pierced the drifting fog to

illuminate a nearby gravestone. Artie bent down to examine the inscription.

THOMAS DOCHERTY
COAL MERCHANT

BORN 1757
DIED 1808

REQUIESCAT IN PACE

He straightened up and translated the three Latin words at the end. "Rest in peace." Artie paused thoughtfully. "Ham, do you never wonder what comes after – you know, beyond the grave?"

"I do not," Ham stated firmly. "I expect I'll find that out when the time comes and not before."

"Keep moving," Artie suggested. "That will warm you up. And keep your eyes peeled."

"Peeled? Peeled for what?"

"Well, ghosts for one thing. If we actually saw a ghost that would be proof, wouldn't it, that something lies beyond?"

Ham shuddered. "Listen, if we run into a ghost, you can ask him all the questions you want about what they do on the other side, what they have for tea and suchlike. Me – I'll be gone as fast as a hare with its tail on fire."

"You wouldn't just leave me here to face a ghost alone, would you?"

"I would," Ham answered flatly. "It's not like when I helped you in that fight with the barrow boys. I doubt you can land a punch on a ghost."

"Well, if we can't harm them, it stands to reason that they can't hurt us either."

"Reason has nothing to do with it," Ham asserted firmly. "People have been running away from ghosts for hundreds of years and I don't intend to break with tradition."

Artie made an exasperated noise and walked on.

Just then Ham seized his forearm. Artie saw that his friend's eyes had grown wide with horror and when he followed Ham's gaze his own heartbeat quickened.

Through the sheets of fog he could just make out a figure standing below the bare, skeletal branches of a hawthorn tree. He grabbed Ham by the shoulder and pulled him down behind the nearest gravestone. They crouched there, raising their heads just enough to peep over the top of the stone.

Shrouded in a grey hood and cloak, the apparition drifted slowly across the churchyard. No face could be seen beneath the shadow of the hood, but the two pale, slender hands clutching the cloak tightly in place gave Artie the impression that the spectre was female. Occasionally it paused by a grave before continuing its progress across the kirkyard.

"The Lady in Grey!" said Ham in a choked whisper. "They say she died a hundred years ago upon hearing the news that the man she loved had been killed in battle. Now she wanders the churchyards of Edinburgh searching for his grave."

As the cloaked figure drew closer, the two boys shrank down lower behind the gravestone. Keeping as still as stone themselves, they held their breath, counting the seconds as the eerie stranger drifted past. At last Artie dared a glimpse and caught sight of her fading into the fog. He stood up.

"Come on, let's follow."

Ham held back. "Let her go! For all we know, it might be a demon hiding under that hood."

"Come on!" urged Artie. "We don't want to lose her."

Even as he spoke, a fresh billow of fog rolled over them and the Lady in Grey disappeared in the gloom. Artie strained his eyes until they ached but could see no trace of the ghostly figure.

Aarrooooooo!

Suddenly, from somewhere in the distance, they heard a terrible howling. It shook the winter air, like a cry of inhuman grief.

The two boys froze in their tracks.

"What was that?" Ham quavered, his round face turning white. "A wolf?"

Artie felt his own blood running cold. "There are no wolves in Scotland any more."

"Then it must have been some sort of a monster." Ham's voice cracked with fear. "I've had enough, Artie. I'm getting out of here. Now." He stumbled off in what he hoped was the direction of the gateway.

Artie had no mind to argue.

"It's this way," he said, hurrying after his friend and giving Ham's elbow a tug to steer him in the right direction.

"I really wish you hadn't thrown my bun away," Ham groaned. "I could do with a bit of comfort right now."

The words were no sooner out of his mouth than he tripped over a small grave marker and pitched forward to land flat on his face.

"Ham, are you all right?" cried Artie, kneeling down beside his friend.

Ham didn't speak. His eyes were fixed on a muddy patch of ground just beyond the end of his nose. Slowly he pushed himself up.

"Artie, look at this. Look!"

Artie leaned forward and squinted at the marks on the muddy ground. "It looks like an animal's passed this way," he gasped.

"Do you suppose…" Ham got to his feet and gazed nervously about him. "Do you suppose it was the ghost of Greyfriars Bobby?"

Artie shook his head in numb disbelief. "No terrier made these marks," he said breathlessly. "These are the footprints of a gigantic hound!"

The adventure continues in:

Artie Conan Doyle
and the
Gravediggers' Club

Book 2 in The World's Gone Loki trilogy

Lewis and Greg's old enemy Loki (Norse god of mischief – dodgy green suit) is back, and he's determined to conquer the universe. To stop him, the boys and their friend Susie must make a dimension-jumping journey from snowy St Andrews to Asgard, the City of the Gods.

Luckily, Thor, the god of thunder, has turned up to help them. Unfortunately, he's locked in the boys' garage…

 Also available as an eBook

DiscoverKelpies.co.uk

Book 3 in The World's Gone Loki trilogy

This time, wise-cracking, havoc-wreaking Loki has stolen St Andrews, locked up Odin, and much more besides…

The fate of the town, and indeed the ENTIRE UNIVERSE, rests with our reluctant heroes, Lewis and Greg, and their friend Susie. Can they rescue Odin and outfox troublesome Loki before he destroys the world?

 Also available as an eBook

DiscoverKelpies.co.uk